This Book Belongs To

D1429359

Serena

from Auntie Ena
Xmas 1985

Her beauty was so dazzling, that the courtiers all bowed low before her

HANS CHRISTIAN ANDERSEN'S
FAIRY TALES

A Purnell de luxe classic

Hans Christian Andersen's Fairy Tales

Illustrations by
JENNY THORNE

PURNELL

ISBN 0 361 03870 4

Illustrations © copyright 1977 Purnell Publishers Limited.

First published in this edition 1977 by Purnell Books,

Paulton, Bristol BS18 5LQ, a member of the BPCC Group.

Made and printed in Germany

Reprinted 1978, 1983, 1984

CONTENTS

INTRODUCTION

Once upon a time, in the spring of 1805, a son was born to a poor shoemaker and his wife in the town of Odense in Denmark. He was christened Hans Christian, and from his earliest years his father read stories to him.

All three lived in a single room filled with the shoemaker's tools, one great bed, and Hans' crib. But the walls were hung with pictures, and over the workshop was a shelf with books and songs.

Many years later Hans was to describe this room and the little kitchen with its shining plates. And in his wonderful story, "The Snow Queen", he draws upon the memory he had of the ladder by which his parents could climb to the loft and so out on to the roof where, in the rain gutter, there stood a large box full of earth. It was the only garden his mother possessed and in it she grew kitchen herbs.

Hans Christian Andersen was an awkward, dreamy boy with gentle eyes and a head of hair nearly yellow in colour so fair was it. He had no friends but was content to fill his days with the puppets his father made for him, arranging them and re-arranging them in his toy theatre. Sometimes he would wander aimlessly through the forest, his head full of the latest story his father had told him, or the latest play he had managed to read for himself.

On the death of his father, his mother was forced to go out washing for people, and Hans was left to himself more than ever. Then she married again, and though Hans was convinced that a good fairy would step in and mend his fortunes, his new stepfather had more practical ideas. "Hans," said he, "you must learn a trade."

This was reasonable enough, but at fourteen Hans could think only of the theatre—the Royal Theatre in Copenhagen to be more exact. His mother, loving him as she did, was finally persuaded to let him go, and so into a small bundle went all his possessions.

Hans, until then, had never owned a coat, far less a pair of boots, but now he was equipped with both, and the louder his boots squeaked the more delighted he was, for then he was certain people would notice them.

The parting with his mother must have been very hard for they loved each other tenderly, and though Hans was not to know it, he was never to see her again for she died the following year and was buried in a pauper's grave.

With his huge hat, several sizes too big for him and always tumbling about his ears, his threadbare clothes and his squeaky boots, Hans was not a very acceptable figure when, on his first day in Copenhagen, he presented himself at the Royal Theatre; it was not surprising, therefore, that he was turned away. Then followed two of the hardest years of his young life when, often penniless, he roamed the streets of that beautiful city. But there was something about the shy, awkward boy which attracted the attention of men in authority.

For a time he was befriended by a Professor of music who helped him to study singing, and during this period Hans wrote plays for his beloved theatre, none of which were accepted. But at least his efforts brought him to the notice of one of the theatre's directors,

Jonas Collin, to whom, as he says, he owed all the good fortune that was waiting for him just around the corner. Collin was the fairy godmother in Hans Christian's life. Through him he became a student with the chance of educating himself beyond his wildest dreams, and he was adopted by the whole Collin family.

Still tongue-tied and clumsy in the presence of adults, Hans soon found that he had a captive audience for his wonderful tales in the children of his friends, and he became, as he says, a much sought-after baby-sitter!

In 1835 he published his first book of fairy stories, and those were so eagerly read that others followed. Many of his tales were based on stories and legends he had heard long ago from the ancients in Odense; but his most famous of all, "The Ugly Duckling", was really the story of his own life, and how thankful we are as we read it that it had such a happy ending!

As more and more of his books appeared, Hans Christian Andersen found honours heaped upon him. He was a welcome guest in the houses of the famous and was received by royalty. But among all his new friends, two gave him particular pleasure; these were the Brothers Grimm, William and Jacob, who not only listened to his readings, but offered him their kindly criticism and advice.

Success did not spoil Hans—if anything he became more tender-hearted, more understanding and considerate of others, and when he died in 1875, he was mourned the world over as a great man and a prince of fairy tales.

JANE CARRUTH

COLOUR PLATES

Hans Christian Andersen's Fairy Tales

THE WILD SWANS

FAR hence, in a country whither the swallows fly in our winter-time, there dwelt a King who had eleven sons and one daughter, the beautiful Elise. The eleven brothers (they were princes) went to school with stars on their breasts and swords by their sides; they wrote on golden tablets with diamond pens, and could read either with a book or without one; in short, it was easy to perceive that they were princes. Their sister Elise used to sit upon a little glass stool, and had a picture-book which had cost the half of a kingdom. Oh! the children were so happy! But happy they were not to remain always.

Their father the King married a very wicked Queen, who was not at all kind to the poor children; they found this out on the first day after the marriage, when there was a grand gala at the palace; for when the children played at receiving company, instead of having as many cakes and sweetmeats as they liked, the Queen gave them only some sand in a little dish, and told them to imagine that was something nice.

The week after, she sent the little Elise to be brought up by some peasants in the country, and it was not long before she told the King so many falsehoods about the poor princes that he would have nothing more to do with them at all.

"Away, out into the world, and take care of yourselves," said the wicked Queen; "fly away in the form of great speechless birds." But she could not make their transformation so disagreeable as she wished,—the Princes were changed into eleven white swans. Sending forth a strange cry, they flew out of the palace windows, over the park and over the wood.

It was still early in the morning when they passed by the place where Elise lay sleeping in the peasant's cottage; they flew several times round the roof, stretched their long necks, and flapped their wings, but no one either heard or saw them, they were forced to fly away, up to the clouds and into the wide world; so on they went to the forest which extended as far as the seashore.

The poor little Elise stood in the peasant's cottage amusing herself with a green leaf, for she had no other plaything. She pricked a hole in the leaf and peeped through it at the sun, and then she fancied she saw her brothers' bright eyes, and whenever the warm sunbeams shone full upon her cheeks, she thought of her brothers' kisses.

One day passed exactly like the other. When the wind blew through the thick hedge of rose-trees in front of the house, she would whisper to the roses, "Who is more beautiful than you?" but the roses would shake their heads and say, "Elise." And when the peasant's wife sat on Sundays at the door of her cottage reading her hymn-book, the wind would rustle in the leaves and say to the book, "Who is more pious than thou?"—"Elise," replied the hymn-book. And what the roses and the hymn-book said, was no more than the truth.

Elise was now fifteen years old; she was sent for home; but when the Queen saw how beautiful she was, she hated her the more, and would willingly have transformed her like her brothers into a wild swan, but she dared not do so, because the King wished to see his daughter.

So the next morning the Queen went into a bath which was made of marble, and fitted up with soft pillows and the gayest carpets; she took three toads, kissed them, and said to one, "Settle thou upon Elise's head that she may become dull and sleepy like thee."—"Settle thou upon her forehead," said she to another, "and let her become ugly like thee, so that her father may not know her again."—And "Do thou place thyself upon her bosom," whispered she to the third, "that her heart may become corrupt and evil, a torment to herself." She then put the toads into the clear water, which was immediately tinted with a green colour, and having called Elise, took off her clothes and made her get into the bath—one toad settled among her hair, another on her forehead, and the third upon her bosom, but Elise seemed not at all aware of it, she rose up and three poppies were seen swimming on the water. Had not the animals been poisonous and kissed by a witch, they would have been changed into roses whilst they remained on Elise's head and heart,—she was too good for magic to have any power over her. When the Queen perceived this, she rubbed walnut juice all over the maiden's skin, so that it became quite swarthy, smeared a nasty salve over her lovely face, and entangled her long thick hair,—it was impossible to recognise the beautiful Elise after this.

When her father saw her, he was shocked and said she could not be his daughter; no one would have anything to do with her but the mastiff and the swallows; but they, poor things, could not say anything in her favour.

Poor Elise wept, and thought of her eleven brothers, not one of whom she saw at the palace. In great distress she stole away and wandered the whole day over fields and moors, till she reached the forest. She knew not where to go, but she was so sad, and longed so much to see her brothers, who had been driven out into the world, that she determined to seek and find them.

She had not been long in the forest when night came on, and she lost her way amid the darkness. So she lay down on the soft moss, said her evening prayer, and leaned her head against the trunk of a tree. It was so still in the forest, the air was mild, and from the grass and moss around gleamed the green light of many hundred glowworms, and when Elise lightly touched one of the branches hanging over her, bright insects fell down upon her like falling stars.

All the night long she dreamed of her brothers. They were all children again, played together, wrote with diamond pens upon golden tablets, and looked at the pictures in the beautiful book which had cost half a kingdom. But they did not as formerly make straight strokes and pothooks upon the tablets; no, they wrote of the bold actions they had performed, and the strange adventures they had encountered, and in the picture-book every thing seemed alive, the birds sang, then men and women stepped from the book and talked to Elise and her brothers; however, when she turned over the leaves, they jumped back into their places, so that the pictures did not get confused together.

When Elise awoke the sun was already high in the heavens. She could not see it certainly, for the tall trees of the forest entwined their thickly-leaved branches closely together, which, as the sunbeams played upon them, looked like a golden veil waving to and fro. And the air was so fragrant, and the birds perched upon Elise's shoulders. She heard the noise of water; there were several springs forming a pool, with the prettiest pebbles at the bottom, bushes were growing thickly round, but the deer had trodden a broad path through them, and by this path Elise went down to the water's edge. The water was so clear that had not the boughs and bushes around been moved to and fro by the wind, you might have fancied they were painted upon the smooth surface, so distinctly was each little leaf mirrored upon it, whether glowing in the sunlight or lying in the shade.

As soon as Elise saw her face reflected in the water she was quite startled, so brown and ugly did it look; however, when she wetted her little hand, and rubbed her brow and eyes, the white skin again appeared.—So Elise took off her clothes, stepped into the fresh water, and in the whole world there was not a king's daughter more beautiful than she then appeared.

After she had again dressed herself, and had braided her long hair, she went to the bubbling spring, drank out of the hollow of her hand, and then wandered farther into the forest. She knew not where she was going, but she thought of her brothers, and of the good God who, she felt, would never forsake her. He it was who made the wild crab-trees grow in order to feed the hungry, and who showed her a tree whose boughs bent under the weight of their fruit. She made her noonday meal under its shade, propped up the boughs, and then walked on amid the dark twilight of the forest. It was so still that she could hear her own footsteps, and the rustling of each little withered leaf that was crushed beneath her feet; not a bird was to be seen, not a single sunbeam penetrated through the thick foliage, and the tall stems of the trees stood so close together, that when she looked straight before her, she seemed enclosed by trellis-work upon trellis-work. Oh! there was a solitariness in this forest such as Elise had never known before.

And the night was so dark! not a single glowworm sent forth its light. Sad and melancholy she lay down to sleep, and then it seemed to her as though the boughs above her opened, and that she saw the Angel of God looking down upon her with gentle aspect, and a thousand little cherubs all around him. When she awoke in the morning she could not tell whether this was a dream, or whether she had really been so watched.

She walked on a little farther and met an old woman with a basket full of berries; the old woman gave her some of them, and Elise asked if she had not seen eleven princes ride through the wood.

"No," said the old woman, "but I saw yesterday eleven Swans with golden crowns on their heads swim down the brook near this place."

And she led Elise on a little farther to a precipice, the base of which was washed by a brook; the trees on each side stretched their long leafy branches towards each other, and where they could not

She knew not where she was going

unite, the roots had disengaged themselves from the earth and hung their interlaced fibres over the water.

Elise bade the old woman farewell, and wandered by the side of the stream till she came to the place where it reached the open sea.

The great, the beautiful sea lay extended before the maiden's eyes, but not a ship, not a boat was to be seen; how was she to go on? She observed the numberless little stones on the shore, all of which the waves had washed into a round form; glass, iron, stone, everything that lay scattered there, had been moulded into shape, and yet the water which had effected this was much softer than Elise's delicate, little hand. "It rolls on unweariedly," said she, "and subdues what is so hard; I will be no less unwearied! Thank you for the lesson you have given me, ye bright rolling waves; some day, my heart tells me, you shall carry me to my dear brothers!"

There lay upon the wet sea-grass eleven white swan feathers; Elise collected them together; drops of water hung about them, whether dew or tears she could not tell. She was quite alone on the sea-shore, but she did not care for that, the sea presented an eternal variety to her, more indeed in a few hours than the gentle inland waters would have offered in a whole year. When a black cloud passed over the sky, it seemed as if the sea would say, "I too can look dark," and then the wind would blow and the waves fling out their white foam, but when the clouds shone with a bright red tint, and the winds were asleep, the sea also became like a rose-leaf in hue; it was now green, now white, but as it reposed peacefully, a slight breeze on the shore caused the water to heave gently like the bosom of a sleeping child.

At sunset Elise saw eleven Wild Swans with golden crowns on their heads fly towards the land; they flew one behind another, looking like a streaming white ribbon. Elise climbed the precipice, and concealed herself behind a bush; the swans settled close to her, and flapped their long white wings.

19

As the sun sank beneath the water, the swans also vanished, and in their place stood eleven handsome princes, the brothers of Elise. She uttered a loud cry, for although they were very much altered, Elise knew that they were, felt that they must be, her brothers; she ran into their arms, called them by their names—and how happy were *they* to see and recognise their sister, who was now grown so tall and so beautiful! They laughed and wept, and soon told each other how wickedly their step-mother had acted towards them.

"We," said the eldest of the brothers, "fly or swim as long as the sun is above the horizon, but when it sinks below, we appear again in our human form; we are therefore obliged to look out for a safe resting-place, for if at sunset we were flying among the clouds, we should fall down as soon as we resumed our own form. We do not dwell here, a land quite as beautiful as this lies on the opposite side of the sea, but it is far off,—to reach it, we have to cross the deep waters, and there is no island midway on which we may rest at night; one little solitary rock rises from the waves, and upon it we only just find room enough to stand side by side. There we spend the night in our human form, and when the sea is rough, we are sprinkled by its foam; but we are thankful for this resting-place, for without it we should never be able to visit our dear native country. Only once in the year is this visit to the home of our fathers permitted; we require two of the longest days for our flight, and can remain here only eleven days, during which time we fly over the large forest, whence we can see the palace in which we were born, where our father dwells, and the tower of the church in which our mother was buried. Here even the trees and bushes seem of kin to us, here the wild horses still race over the plains, as in the days of our childhood, here the charcoal-burner still sings the same old tunes to which we used to dance in our youth, here we are still attracted, and here we have found thee, thou dear little sister! We have yet two days longer to stay here, then we must fly over the sea to a land beautiful indeed, but not our fatherland. How shall we take thee with us? we have neither ship nor boat!"

"How shall I be able to release you?" said the sister. And so they went on talking almost the whole of the night. They slumbered only a few hours.

Elise was awakened by the rustling of swans' wings which were fluttering above her. Her brothers were again transformed, and for some time flew around in large circles. At last they flew far, far away; one of them remained behind; it was the youngest. He laid his head in her lap and she stroked his white wings; they remained the whole day together. Towards evening the others came back, and when the sun was set, again they stood on the firm ground in their natural form.

"To-morrow we shall fly away, and may not return for a year, but we cannot leave thee; hast thou courage to accompany us? My arm is strong enough to bear thee through the forest; shall we not have sufficient strength in our wings to transport thee over the sea?"

"Yes, take me with you," said Elise. They spent the whole night in weaving a mat of the pliant willow bark and the tough rushes, and their mat was thick and strong. Elise lay down upon it, and when the sun had risen, and the brothers were again transformed into wild swans, they seized the mat with their beaks and flew up high among the clouds with their dear sister who was still sleeping. The sun-beams shone full upon her face, so one of the swans flew over her head, and shaded her with his broad wings.

They were already far from land when Elise awoke: she thought she was still dreaming, so strange did it appear to her to be travelling through the air, and over the sea. By her side lay a cluster of pretty berries, and a handful of savoury roots. Her youngest brother had collected and laid them there; and she thanked him with a smile, for she knew him as the swan who flew over her head and shaded her with his wings.

They flew so high, that the first ship they saw beneath them seemed like a white sea-gull hovering over the water. Elise saw behind her a large cloud; it looked like a mountain, and on it she saw the gigantic shadows of herself and the eleven swans—it formed a picture more splendid than any she had ever yet seen; soon, however, the sun rose higher, the cloud remained far behind, and then the floating shadowy picture disappeared.

The whole day they continued flying with a whizzing noise somewhat like an arrow, but yet they went slower than usual—they had their sister to carry. A heavy tempest was gathering, the evening approached; anxiously did Elise watch the sun, it was setting, still the solitary rock could not be seen; it appeared to her that the swans plied their wings with increasing vigour. Alas! it would be her fault if her brothers did not arrive at the place in time! they would become human beings when the sun set, and if this happened before they reached the rock, they must fall into the sea and be drowned. She prayed to God most fervently; still no rock was to be seen, the black clouds drew nearer, violent gusts of wind announced the approach of a tempest, the clouds rested perpendicularly upon a fearfully large wave which rolled quickly forwards, and one flash of lightning rapidly succeeded another.

The sun was now on the rim of the sea. Elise's heart beat violently; the swans shot downwards so swiftly that she thought she must fall, but again they began to hover; the sun was half sunk beneath the water, and at that moment she saw the little rock below her; it looked like a seal's head when he raises it just above the water. And the sun was sinking fast,—it seemed scarcely larger than a star,—her foot touched the hard ground, and it vanished altogether, like the last spark on a burnt piece of paper. Arm in arm stood her brothers around her; there was only just room for her and them—the sea beat tempestuously against the rock, flinging over them a shower of foam; the sky seemed in a continual blaze with the fast-succeeding flashes of fire that lightened it, and peal after peal rolled on the thunder, but sister and brothers kept firm hold of each other's hands. They sang a psalm, and their psalm gave them comfort and courage.

By daybreak the air was pure and still, and as soon as the sun rose, the swans flew away with Elise from the rock. The waves rose higher and higher, and when they looked from the clouds down upon the blackish-green sea, covered as it was with white foam, they might have fancied that millions of swans were swimming on its surface.

As day advanced, Elise saw floating in the air before her a land of mountains intermixed with glaciers, and in the centre a palace a mile in length, with splendid colonnades, surrounded by palm-trees and gorgeous-looking flowers as large as mill-wheels. She asked if this were the country to which they were flying, but the swans shook their heads, for what she saw was the beautiful airy castle of the fairy Morgana, where no human being was admitted; and whilst Elise still bent her eyes upon it, mountains, trees, and castle all disappeared, and in their place stood twelve churches with high towers and pointed windows—she fancied she heard the organ play, but it was only the murmur of the sea. She was now close to these churches, but behold! they had changed into a large fleet sailing under them; she looked down and saw it was only a sea mist passing rapidly over the water. An eternal variety floated before her eyes, till at last the actual land to which she was going appeared in sight. Beautiful blue mountains, cedar woods, towns, and castles rose to view. Long before sunset Elise sat down among the mountains, in front of a large cavern; delicate young creepers grew around so thickly that it appeared covered with gay embroidered carpets.

"Now we shall see what thou wilt dream of to-night!" said her youngest brother, as he showed her the sleeping chamber destined for her.

"Oh that I could dream how you might be released from the spell!" said she; and this thought completely occupied her; she prayed most earnestly for God's assistance, nay, even in her dreams she continued praying, and it appeared to her that she was flying up high in the air towards the castle of the fairy Morgana. The fairy came forward to meet her, radiant and beautiful, and yet she fancied she resembled the old woman who had given her berries in the forest, and told her of the Swans with golden crowns.

"Thou *canst* release thy brothers," said she, "but hast thou courage and patience sufficient? The water is indeed softer than thy delicate hands, and yet can mould the hard stones to its will, but then it cannot feel the pain which thy tender fingers will feel; it has no heart, and cannot suffer the anxiety and grief which thou must suffer. Dost thou see these stinging-nettles which I have in my hand? There are many of the same kind growing round the cave where thou art sleeping; only those that grow there or on the graves in the churchyard are of use, remember that! Thou must pluck them, although they will sting thy hand, thou must trample on the nettles with thy feet, and get yarn from them, and with this yarn thou must weave eleven shirts with long sleeves;—throw them over the eleven wild swans, and the spell is broken. But mark this: from the moment that thou beginnest thy work till it is completed, even should it occupy thee for years, thou must not speak a word; the first syllable that escapes thy lips will fall like a dagger into the hearts of thy brothers; on thy tongue depends their life. Mark well all this!"

And at the same moment the fairy touched Elise's hands with a nettle, which made them burn like fire, and Elise awoke. It was broad daylight, and close to her lay a nettle like the one she had seen in her dream. She fell upon her knees, thanked God, and then went out of the cave in order to begin her work. She plucked with her own delicate hands the disagreeable stinging-nettles; they burned large blisters on her hands and arms, but she bore the pain willingly in the hope of releasing her dear brothers. She trampled on the nettles with her naked feet, and spun the green yarn.

At sunset came her brothers. Elise's silence quite frightened them, they thought it must be the effect of some fresh spell of their wicked step-mother, but when they saw her blistered hands, they found out what their sister was doing for their sakes. The youngest brother wept, and when his tears fell upon her hands, Elise felt no more pain; the blisters disappeared.

The whole night she spent in her work, for she could not rest till she had released her brothers. All the following day she sat in her solitude, for the swans had flown away; but never had time passed so quickly. One shirt was ready; she now began the second.

Suddenly a hunting horn resounded among the mountains. Elise was frightened. The noise came nearer, she heard the hounds barking; in great terror she fled into the cave, bound up the nettles which she had gathered and combed into a bundle, and sat down upon it.

In the same moment a large dog sprang out from the bushes; two others immediately followed, they barked loudly, ran away and then returned. It was not long before the hunters stood in front of the cave; the handsomest among them was the King of that country; he stepped up to Elise. Never had he seen a lovelier maiden.

"How camest thou here, thou beautiful child?" said he. Elise shook her head, she dared not speak, for a word might have cost her the life of her brothers, and she hid her hands under her apron lest the King should see how she was suffering.

"Come with me," said he, "thou must not stay here! If thou art good as thou art beautiful, I will dress thee in velvet and silk, I will put a gold crown upon thy head, and thou shalt dwell in my palace!" So he lifted her upon his horse, while she wept and wrung her hands; but the King said, "I only desire thy happiness! thou shalt thank me for this some day!" and away he rode over mountains and valleys, holding her on his horse in front, whilst the other hunters followed. When the sun set, the King's magnificent capital with its churches and cupolas lay before them, and the King led Elise into the palace, where, in a high marble hall, fountains were playing, and the walls and ceiling displayed the most beautiful paintings. But Elise cared not for all this splendour, she wept and mourned in silence, even whilst some female attendants dressed her in royal robes, wove costly pearls in her hair, and drew soft gloves over her blistered hands.

And now she was full dressed, and as she stood in her splendid attire, her beauty was so dazzling, that the courtiers all bowed low before her, and the King chose her for his bride, although the Archbishop shook his head, and whispered that the "beautiful lady of the wood must certainly be a witch, who had blinded their eyes, and infatuated the King's heart."

But the King did not listen, and ordered that music should be played. A sumptuous banquet was served up, and the loveliest maidens danced round the bride; she was led through fragrant gardens into magnificent halls, but not a smile was seen to play upon her lips or beam from her eyes. The King then opened a small room next her sleeping apartment; it was adorned with costly green tapestry, and exactly resembled the cave in which she had been found; upon the ground lay the bundle of yarn which she had spun from the nettles, and by the wall hung the shirt she had completed. One of the hunters had brought all this, thinking there must be something wonderful in it.

"Here thou mayest dream of thy former home," said the King; "here is the work which employed thee; amidst all thy present splendour it may sometimes give thee pleasure to fancy thyself there again."

When Elise saw what was so dear to her heart, she smiled, and the blood returned to her cheeks; she thought her brothers might still be released, and she kissed the King's hand; he pressed her to his heart and ordered the bells of all the churches in the city be rung, to announce the celebration of their wedding. The beautiful dumb maiden of the wood was to become Queen of the land.

The Archbishop whispered evil words in the King's ear, but they made no impression upon him; the marriage was solemnised, and the Archbishop himself was obliged to put the crown upon her head. In his rage he pressed the narrow rim so firmly on her forehead that it hurt her; but a heavier weight (sorrow for her brothers) lay upon her heart; she did not feel bodily pain. She was still silent, a single word would have killed her brothers; her eyes, however, beamed with heartfelt love to the King, so good and handsome, who had done so much to make her happy. She became more warmly attached to him every day. Oh! how much she wished she might confide to him all her sorrows! but she was forced to remain silent, she could not speak until her work was completed! To this end she stole away every night, and went into the little room that was fitted up in imitation of the cave; there she worked at her shirts, but by the time she had begun the seventh, all her yarn was spent.

She knew that the nettles she needed grew in the churchyard, but she must gather them herself; how was she to get them?

"Oh, what is the pain in my fingers compared to the anguish my heart suffers!" thought she. "I must venture to the churchyard; the good God will not withdraw His protection from me!"

Fearful as though she was about to do something wrong, one moonlight night she crept down to the garden, and through the long avenues got into the lonely road leading to the churchyard. She saw sitting on one of the broadest tombstones a number of ugly old witches. They took off their ragged clothes as if they were going to bathe, and digging with their long lean fingers into the fresh grass, drew up the dead bodies and devoured the flesh. Elise was obliged to pass close by them, and the witches fixed their wicked eyes upon her; but she repeated her prayer, gathered the stinging-nettles, and took them back with her into the palace. One person only had seen her; it was the Archbishop, who was awake when others slept; now he was convinced that all was not right about the Queen; she must be a witch, who had through her enchantments infatuated the King, and all the people.

In the Confessional he told the King what he had seen, and what he feared; and when the slanderous words came from his lips, the sculptured images of the saints shook their heads as though they would say, "It is untrue, Elise is innocent!" But the Archbishop explained the omen quite otherwise; he thought it was a testimony against her that the holy images shook their heads at hearing of her sin.

Two large tears rolled down the King's cheeks; he returned home in doubt, he pretended to sleep at night, though sleep never visited him; and he noticed that Elise rose from her bed every night, and every time he followed her secretly and saw her enter her little room.

His countenance became darker every day; Elise perceived it, though she knew not the cause. She was much pained, and besides, what did she not suffer in her heart for her brothers! Her bitter tears ran down on the royal velvet and purple; they looked like bright diamonds, and all who saw the magnificence that surrounded her, wished themselves in her place. She had now nearly finished her work, only one shirt was wanting; unfortunately, yarn was wanting also, she had not a single nettle left. Once more, only this one time, she must go to the churchyard and gather a few handfuls. She shuddered when she thought of the solitary walk and of the horrid witches, but her resolution was as firm as her trust in God.

Elise went, the King and the Archbishop followed her; they saw her disappear at the churchyard door, and when they came nearer, they saw the witches sitting on the tombstones as Elise had seen them, and the King turned away, for he believed her whose head had rested on his bosom that very evening to be amongst them. "Let the people judge her!" said he. And the people condemned her to be burnt.

She was now dragged from the King's sumptuous apartments into a dark, damp prison, where the wind whistled through the grated window. Instead of velvet and silk, they gave her the bundle of nettles she had gathered; on that must she lay her head, the shirts she had woven must serve her as mattress and counterpane;—but they could not have given her anything she valued so much; and she continued her work, at the same time praying earnestly to her God. The boys sang scandalous songs about her in front of her prison; not a soul comforted her with one word of love.

Towards evening she heard the rustling of swan's wings at the grating. It was the youngest of her brothers, who had at last found his sister, and she sobbed aloud for joy although she knew that the coming night would probably be the last of her life; but then her work was almost finished and her brother was near.

The Archbishop came in order to spend the last hour with her; he had promised the King he would; but she shook her head and entreated him with her eyes and gestures to go—this night she must finish her work, or all she had suffered, her pain, her anxiety, her sleepless nights, would be in vain. The Archbishop went away with many angry words, but the unfortunate Elise knew herself to be perfectly innocent, and went on with her work.

Little mice ran busily about and dragged the nettles to her feet, wishing to help her; and the thrush perched on the iron bars of the window, and sang all night as merrily as he could, that Elise might not lose courage.

It was still twilight, just one hour before sunrise, when the eleven brothers stood before the palace gates, requesting an audience with the King; but it could not be, they were told, it was still night, the King was asleep, and they dared not wake him. They entreated, they threatened, the guard came up, the King himself at last stepped out to ask what was the matter,—at that moment the sun rose, the brothers could be seen no longer, and eleven white Swans flew away over the palace.

The people poured forth from the gates of the city; they wished to see the witch burnt. One wretched horse drew the cart in which Elise was placed. A coarse frock of sackcloth had been put on her, her beautiful long hair hung loosely over her shoulders, her cheeks were of a deadly paleness, her lips moved gently, and her fingers wove the green yarn: even on her way to her cruel death she did not give up her work; the ten shirts lay at her feet, she was now labouring to complete the eleventh. The rabble insulted her.

"Look at the witch, how she mutters! she has not a hymn-book in her hand, no, there she sits with her accursed hocuspocus. Tear it from her, tear it into a thousand pieces!"

And they all crowded about her, and were on the point of snatching away the shirts, when eleven white Swans came flying towards the cart; they settled all round her, and flapped their wings. The crowd gave way in terror.

"It is a sign from Heaven; she is certainly innocent!" whispered some; they dared not say so aloud.

The Sheriff now seized her by the hand—in a moment she threw the eleven shirts over the Swans, and eleven handsome Princes appeared in their place. The youngest had, however, only one arm, and a wing instead of the other, for one sleeve was deficient in his shirt; it had not been quite finished.

"Now I may speak," said she: "I am innocent!"

And the people who had seen what had happened bowed before her as before a saint. She, however, sank lifeless in her brothers' arms; suspense, fear, and grief had quite exhausted her.

"Yes, she is innocent," said her eldest brother, and he now related their wonderful history. Whilst he spoke a fragrance as delicious as though it proceeded from millions of roses diffused itself around, for every piece of wood in the funeral pile had taken root and sent forth branches, a hedge of blooming red roses surrounded Elise, and above all the others blossomed a flower of dazzling white colour, bright as a star; the King plucked it and laid it on Elise's bosom, whereupon she awoke from her trance with peace and joy in her heart.

And all the church bells began to ring of their own accord, and birds flew to the spot in swarms, and there was a festive procession back to the palace, such as no King has ever seen equalled.

THE UGLY DUCKLING

It was beautiful in the country; it was summer-time, the wheat was yellow, the oats were green, the hay was stacked up in the green meadows, and the stork paraded about on his long red legs, discoursing in Egyptian, which language he had learned from his mother. The fields and meadows were skirted by thick woods, and a deep lake lay in the midst of the woods.—Yes, it was indeed beautiful in the country! The sunshine fell warmly on an old mansion, surrounded by deep canals, and from the walls down to the water's edge there grew large burdock-leaves, so high that children could stand upright among them without being perceived. This place was as wild and unfrequented as the thickest part of the wood, and on that account a duck had chosen to make her nest there. She was sitting on her eggs; but the pleasure she had felt at first was now almost gone, because she had been there so long, and had so few visitors, for the other ducks preferred swimming on the canals to sitting among the burdock-leaves gossiping with her.

At last the eggs cracked one after another, "Tchick, tchick!" All the eggs were alive, and one little head after another appeared. "Quack, quack," said the duck, and all got up as well as they could; they peeped about from under the green leaves, and as green is good for the eyes, their mother let them look as long as they pleased.

"How large the world is!" said the little ones, for they found their present situation very different to their former confined one, while yet in the egg-shells.

"Do you imagine this to be the whole of the world?" said the mother! "it extends far beyond the other side of the garden, to the pastor's field; but I have never been there. Are you all here?" And then she got up. "No, I have not got you all, the largest egg is still here. How long will this last?" And then she sat down again.

"Well, and how are you getting on?" asked an old duck.

"This one egg keeps me so long," said the mother, "it will not break; but you should see the others! they are the prettiest little ducklings I have seen in all my days; they are all like their father,— the good-for-nothing fellow! he has not been to visit me once."

"Let me see the egg that will not break," said the old duck, "depend upon it, it is a turkey's egg. I was cheated in the same way once myself, and I had such trouble with the young ones; for they were afraid of the water, and I could not get them there. I called and scolded, but it was all of no use. But let me see the egg—ah yes! to be sure, that is a turkey's egg. Leave it, and teach the other little ones to swim."

"I will sit on it a little longer," said the duck. "I have been sitting so long, that I may as well spend the harvest here."

"It is no business of mine," said the old duck, and away she waddled.

The great egg burst at last, "Tchick, tchick," said the little one, and out it tumbled—but oh! how large and ugly it was! The duck looked at it, "That is a great, strong creature," said she, "none of the others are at all like it, can it be a young turkey-cock? well, we shall soon find out, it must go into the water, though I push it in myself."

The next day there was delightful weather, and the sun shone warmly upon all the green leaves when mother duck with all her family went down to the canal; plump she went into the water, "quack, quack," cried she, and one duckling after another jumped in. The water closed over their heads, but all came up again, and swam together in the pleasantest manner; their legs moved without effort. All were there, even the ugly, grey one.

"No! it is not a turkey," said the old duck; "only see how prettily it moves its legs, how upright it holds itself, it is my own child! it is also really very pretty when one looks more closely at it; quack, quack, now come with me.

I will take you into the world, introduce you in the duckyard; but keep close to me, or some one may tread on you, and beware of the cat."

"I almost wish it could be hatched over again."

So they came into the duckyard. There was a horrid noise; two families were quarreling about the remains of an eel, which in the end was secured by the cat.

"See, my children, such is the way of the world," said the mother duck, wiping her beak, for she too was found of roasted eels. "Now use your legs," said she, "keep together, and bow to the old duck you see yonder. She is the most distinguished of all the fowls present, and is of Spanish blood, which accounts for her dignified appearance and manners. And look, she has a red rag on her leg; that is considered extremely handsome, and is the greatest distinction a duck can have.

"Don't turn your feet inwards, a well-educated duckling always keeps his legs far apart, like his father and mother, just so—look! now bow your necks, and say 'quack.' "

And they did as they were told. But the other ducks who were in the yard looked at them and said aloud, "Only see, now we have another brood, as if there were not enough of us already, and fie! how ugly that one is, we will not endure it," and immediately one of the ducks flew at him, and bit him in the neck.

"Leave him alone," said the mother, "he is doing no one any harm."

"Yes, but he is so large, and so strange-looking, and therefore he shall be teased."

"Those are fine children that our good mother has," said the old duck with the red rag on her leg. "All are pretty except one, and that has not turned out well; I almost wish it could be hatched over again."

"That cannot be, please your highness," said the mother. "Certainly he is not handsome, but he is a very good child, and swims as well as the others, indeed rather better. I think he will grow like the others all in good time, and perhaps will look smaller. He stayed so long in the egg-shell, that is the cause of the difference," and she scratched the duckling's neck, and stroked his whole body. "Besides," added she, "he is a drake; I think he will be very strong, therefore it does not matter so much, he will fight his way through."

"The other ducks are very pretty," said the old duck; "pray make yourselves at home, and if you find an eel's head you can bring it to me."

And accordingly they made themselves at home.

But the poor little duckling, who had come last out of its egg-shell, and who was so ugly, was bitten, pecked, and teased by both ducks and hens. "It is so large," said they all. And the turkey-cock, who had come into the world with spurs on, and therefore fancied he was an emperor, puffed himself up like a ship in full sail, and marched up to the duckling quite red with passion. The poor little thing scarcely knew what to do; he was quite distressed, because he was so ugly, and because he was the jest of the poultry yard.

So passed the first day, and afterwards matters grew worse and worse; the poor duckling was scorned by all. Even his brothers and sisters behaved unkindly, and were constantly saying, "The cat fetch thee, thou nasty creature!" The mother said, "Ah, if thou wert only far away!" The ducks bit him, the hens pecked him, and the girl who fed the poultry kicked him. He ran over the hedge; the little birds in the bushes were terrified. "That is because I am so ugly," thought the duckling, shutting his eyes, but he ran on. At last he came to a wide moor, where lived some wild ducks; here he lay the whole night, so tired and so comfortless. In the morning the wild ducks flew up, and perceived their new companion. "Pray who are you?" asked they; and our little duckling turned himself in all directions, and greeted them as politely as possible.

"You are really uncommonly ugly," said the wild duck; "however that does not matter to us, provided you do not marry into our families." Poor thing! he had never thought of marrying; he only begged permission to lie among the reeds, and drink the water of the moor.

There he lay for two whole days—on the third day there came two wild geese, or rather ganders, who had not been long out of

"You are really uncommonly ugly."

their egg-shells, which accounts for their impertinence.

"Hark-ye," said they, "you are so ugly that we like you infinitely well; will you come with us, and be a bird of passage? On another moor, not far from this, are some dear, sweet, wild geese, as lovely creatures as have ever said 'hiss, hiss'. You are truly in the way to make your fortune, ugly as you are."

Bang! a gun went off all at once, and both wild geese were stretched dead among the reeds, the water became red with blood; —bang! a gun went off again, whole flocks of wild geese flew up from among the reeds, and another report followed.

There was a grand hunting party: the hunters lay in ambush all around; some were even sitting in the trees, whose huge branches stretched far over the moor. The blue smoke rose through the thick trees like a mist, and was dispersed as it fell over the water; the hounds splashed about in the mud, the reeds and rushes bent in all directions—how frightened the poor little duck was! he turned his head, thinking to hide it under his wings, and in a moment a most formidable-looking dog stood close to him, his tongue hanging out of his mouth, his eyes sparkling fearfully. He opened wide his jaws at the sight of our duckling, showed him his sharp white teeth, and, splash, splash! he was gone, gone without hurting him.

"Well! let me be thankful," sighed he, "I am so ugly, that even the dog will not eat me."

And now he lay still, though the shooting continued among the reeds, shot following shot.

The noise did not cease till late in the day, and even then the poor little thing dared not stir; he waited several hours before he looked around him, and then hastened away from the moor as fast as he could. He ran over fields and meadows, though the wind was so high that he had some difficulty in proceeding.

Towards evening he reached a wretched little hut, so wretched that it knew not on which side to fall, and therefore remained standing. The wind blew violently, so that our poor little duckling was obliged to support himself on his tail, in order to stand against it; but it became worse and worse. He then remarked that the door had lost one of its hinges, and hung so much awry that he could creep through the crevice into the room, which he did.

In this room lived an old woman, with her tom-cat and her hen; and the cat, whom she called her little son, knew how to set up his back and purr; indeed he could even emit sparks when stroked the wrong way. The hen had very short legs, and was therefore called "Cuckoo Shortlegs"; she laid very good eggs, and the old woman loved her as her own child.

The next morning the new guest was perceived; the cat began to mew, and the hen to cackle.

"What is the matter?" asked the old woman, looking round; however, her eyes were not good, so she took the young duckling to be a fat duck who had lost her way. "This is a capital catch," said she, "I shall now have ducks' eggs, if it be not a drake: we must try."

And so the duckling was put to the proof for three weeks, but no eggs made their appearance.

Now the cat was the master of the house, and the hen was the mistress, and they used always to say, "We and the world," for they imagined themselves to be not only the half of the world, but also by far the better half. The duckling thought it was possible to be of a different opinion, but that the hen would not allow.

"Can you lay eggs?" asked she.

"No."

"Well, then, hold your tongue."

And the cat said, "Can you set up your back? can you purr?"

"No."

"Well, then, you should have no opinion when reasonable persons are speaking."

So the duckling sat alone in the corner, and was in a very bad humour; however, he happened to think of the fresh air and bright sunshine, and these thoughts gave him such a strong desire to swim again that he could not help telling it to the hen.

"What ails you?" said the hen. "You have nothing to do, and, therefore, brood over these fancies; either lay eggs, or purr, then you will forget them."

"But it is so delicious to swim," said the duckling, "so delicious when the waters close over your head, and you plunge to the bottom."

"Well, that is a queer sort of a pleasure!" said the hen. "I think you must be crazy. Not to speak of myself, ask the cat—he is the most sensible animal I know—whether he would like to swim or to plunge to the bottom of the water. Ask our mistress, the old woman— there is no one in the world wiser than she—do you think she would take pleasure in swimming, and in the waters closing over her head?"

"You do not understand me," said the duckling.

"What, we do not understand you! So you think yourself wiser than the cat, and the old woman, not to speak of myself. Do not fancy any such thing, child, but be thankful for all the kindness that has been shown you. Are you not lodged in a warm room, and have you not the advantage of society from which you can learn something? But you are a simpleton, and it is wearisome to have anything to do with you. Believe me, I wish you well. I tell you unpleasant things, but it is thus that real friendship is shown. Come, for once give yourself the trouble to learn to purr, or to lay eggs."

"I think I will go out into the wide world again," said the duckling.

"Well, go," answered the hen.

So the duckling went. He swam on the surface of the water, he plunged beneath, but all animals passed him by, on account of his ugliness. And the autumn came, the leaves turned yellow and brown, the wind caught them and danced them about, the air was very cold, the clouds were heavy with hail or snow, and the raven sat on the hedge and croaked:—the poor duckling was certainly not very comfortable!

One evening, just as the sun was setting with unusual brilliancy, a flock of large beautiful birds rose from out of the brushwood; the duckling had never seen anything so beautiful before; their plumage was of a dazzling white, and they had long, slender necks. They were swans; they uttered a singular cry, spread out their long, splendid wings, and flew away from these cold regions to warmer countries, across the open sea. They flew so high, so very high! and the little ugly duckling's feelings were so strange; he turned round and round in the water like a mill-wheel, strained his neck to look after them, and sent forth such a loud and strange cry, that it almost frightened himself.—Ah! he could not forget them, those noble birds! those happy birds! When he could see them no longer, he plunged to the bottom of the water, and when he rose again, was almost beside himself. The duckling knew not what the birds were called, knew not whither they were flying, yet he loved them as he had never before loved anything; he envied them not, it would never have occurred to him to wish such beauty for himself; he would have been quite contented if the ducks in the duckyard had but endured his company —the poor ugly animal!

And the winter was so cold, so cold! The duckling was obliged to swim round and round in the water, to keep it from freezing; but every night the opening in which he swam became smaller and smaller; it froze so that the crust of ice crackled; the duckling was obliged to make good use of his legs to prevent the water from freezing entirely; at last, wearied out, he lay stiff and cold in the ice.

Early in the morning there passed by a peasant, who saw him, broke the ice in pieces with his wooden shoe, and brought him home to his wife.

He now revived; the children would have played with him, but our duckling thought they wished to tease him, and in his terror jumped into the milk-pail, so that the milk was spilled about the room: the good woman screamed and clapped her hands; he flew thence into the pan where the butter was kept, and thence into the meal-barrel, and out again, and then how strange he looked!

The woman screamed, and struck at him with the tongs, the children ran races with each other trying to catch him, and laughed and screamed likewise. It was well for him that the door stood open; he jumped out among the bushes into the new fallen snow and lay there as in a dream.

But it would be too melancholy to relate all the trouble and misery that he was obliged to suffer during the severity of the winter—he was lying on a moor among the reeds, when the sun began to shine warmly again, the larks sang, and beautiful spring had returned.

And once more he shook his wings. They were stronger than formerly, and bore him forwards quickly, and before he was well aware of it, he was in a large garden where the apple-trees stood in full bloom, where the syringas sent forth their fragrance and hung their long green branches down into the winding canal. Oh! everything was so lovely, so full of the freshness of spring! And out of the thicket came three beautiful white swans. They displayed their feathers so proudly, and swam so lightly, so lightly! The duckling knew the glorious creatures, and was seized with a strange melancholy.

"I will fly to them, those kingly birds!" said he. "They will kill me, because I, ugly as I am, have presumed to approach them; but it matters not; better to be killed by them than to be bitten by the ducks, pecked by the hens, kicked by the girl who feeds the poultry, and to have so much to suffer during the winter!" He flew into the water, and swam towards the beautiful creatures—they saw him and shot forward to meet him. "Only kill me," said the poor animal, and he bowed his head low, expecting death,—but what did he see in the water?—he saw beneath him his own form, no longer that of a plump, ugly, grey bird—it was that of a swan.

It matters not to have been born in a duckyard, if one has been hatched from a swan's egg.

The good creature felt himself really elevated by all the troubles and adversities he had experienced. He could now rightly understand his own happiness, and the larger swans swam round him, and stroked him with their beaks.

Some little children were running about in the garden; they threw grain and bread into the water, and the youngest exclaimed, "There is a new one!" The others also cried out, "Yes, there is a new swan come!" and they clapped their hands, and danced around. They ran to their father and mother, bread and cake were thrown into the water, and every one said, "The new one is the best, so young, and so beautiful!" and the old swans bowed before him. The young swan felt quite ashamed, and hid his head under his wings; he scarcely knew what to do, he was all too happy, but still not proud, for a good heart is never proud.

He remembered how he had been persecuted and derided, and he now heard every one say he was the most beautiful of all beautiful birds. The syringas bent down their branches towards him low into the water, and the sun shone so warmly and brightly—he shook his feathers, stretched his slender neck, and in the joy of his heart said, "How little did I dream of so much happiness when I was the ugly duckling!"

THE NIGHTINGALE

In China, as you well know, the Emperor is Chinese, and all around him are Chinese also.—Now what I am about to relate, happened many years ago, but even on that very account it is the more important that you should hear the story now, before it is forgotten.

The Emperor's palace was the most magnificent palace in the world; it was made entirely of fine porcelain, exceedingly costly; but at the same time so brittle that it was dangerous even to touch it.

The choicest flowers were to be seen in the garden; and to the most splendid of all these little silver bells were fastened, in order that their tinkling might prevent any one from passing by without noticing them. Yes! everything in the Emperor's garden was excellently well arranged; and the garden extended so far that even the gardener did not know the end of it; whoever walked beyond it, however, came to a beautiful wood, with very high trees; and beyond that, to the sea. The wood went down quite to the sea, which was very deep and blue; large ships could sail close under the branches; and among the branches dwelt a nightingale, who sang so sweetly, that even the poor fisherman, who had so much else to do, when he came out at night time to cast his nets, would stand still and listen to her song. "Oh! how pretty that is!" he would say—but then he was obliged to mind his work, and forget the bird; yet the following night, if again the nightingale sang, and the fisherman came out, again he would say, "Oh! how pretty that is!"

Travellers came from all parts of the world to the Emperor's city; and they admired the city, the palace, and the garden; but if they heard the nightingale, they all said, "This is the best." And they talked about her after they went home, and learned men wrote books about the city, the palace, and the garden; nor did they forget the nightingale: she was extolled above everything else; and poets wrote the most beautiful verses about the nightingale of the wood near the sea.

These books went round the world, and one of them at last reached the Emperor. He was sitting in his golden arm-chair; he read and read, and nodded his head every moment; for these splendid descriptions of the city, the palace, and the garden, pleased him greatly. "But the nightingale is the best of all," was written in the book.

"What in the world is this?" said the Emperor. "The nightingale! I do not know it at all! Can there be such a bird in my empire, in my garden even, without my having even heard of it? Truly one may learn something from books."

So he called his Cavalier[1]; now this was so grand a personage that no one of inferior rank might speak to him; and if one did venture

1 Gentleman in waiting.

to ask him a question, his only answer was "Pish!" which has no particular meaning.

"There is said to be a very remarkable bird here, called the nightingale," said the Emperor; "her song, they say, is worth more than anything else in all my dominions; why has no one ever told me of her?"

"I have never before heard her mentioned," said the Cavalier: "she has never been presented at court."

"I wish her to come, and sing before me this evening," said the Emperor. "The whole world knows what I have, and I do not know it myself!"

"I have never before heard her mentioned," said the Cavalier; "but I will seek her, I will find her."

But where was she to be found? The Cavalier ran up one flight of steps, down another, through halls, and through passages; not one of all whom he met had ever heard of the nightingale; and the Cavalier returned to the Emperor, and said, "It must certainly be an invention of the man who wrote the book. Your Imperial Majesty must not believe all that is written in books; much of them is pure invention, and there is what is called the Black Art."

"But the book in which I have read it," said the Emperor, "was sent me by the high and mighty Emperor of Japan, and therefore it cannot be untrue. I wish to hear the nightingale; she must be here this evening, and if she do not come, after supper the whole court shall be flogged."

"Tsing-pe!" said the Cavalier; and again he ran up stairs, and down stairs, through halls, and through passages, and half the court ran with him; for not one would have relished the flogging. Many were the questions asked respecting the wonderful nightingale, whom the whole world talked of, and about whom no one at court knew anything.

At last they met a poor little girl in the kitchen who said, "Oh yes! the nightingale! I know her very well. Oh! how she can sing!

Every evening I carry the fragments left at table to my poor sick mother. She lives by the sea-shore; and when I am coming back, and stay to rest a little in the wood, I hear the nightingale sing; it makes the tears come into my eyes! it is just as if my mother kissed me."

"Little kitchen maiden," said the Cavalier, "I will procure for you a sure appointment in the kitchen, together with permission to see His Majesty the Emperor dine, if you will conduct us to the nightingale, for she is expected at court this evening."

So they went together to the wood, where the nightingale was accustomed to sing; and half the court went with them. Whilst on their way, a cow began to low.

"Oh!" said the court pages "now we have her! It is certainly an extraordinary voice for so small an animal; surely I have heard it somewhere before."

"No, those are cows you hear lowing," said the little kitchen-maid, "we are still far from the place."

The frogs were now croaking in the pond.

"That is famous!" said the chief court-preacher, "now I hear her; it sounds just like little church bells."

"No, those are frogs," said the little kitchen-maid, "but now I think we shall soon hear her."

Then the nightingale began to sing.

"There she is!" said the little girl, "listen! listen! There she sits!" and she pointed to a little grey bird up in the branches.

"Is it possible?" said the Cavalier. "I should not have thought it. How simple she looks! she must certainly have changed colour at the sight of so many distinguished personages."

"Little nightingale!" called out the kitchen-maid, "our gracious Emperor wishes you to sing something to him."

"With the greatest pleasure," said the nightingale, and she sang in such a manner that it was delightful to hear her.

"It sounds like glass bells," said the Cavalier. "And look at her little throat, how it moves! It is singular that we should never have heard her before; she will have great success at court."

"Shall I sing again to the Emperor?" asked the nightingale, for she thought the Emperor was among them.

"Most excellent nightingale!" said the Cavalier, "I have the honour to invite you to a court festival, which is to take place this evening, when his Imperial Majesty will be enchanted with your delightful song."

"My song would sound far better among the green trees," said the nightingale; however she followed willingly when she heard that the Emperor wished it.

There was a regular trimming and polishing at the palace; the walls and the floors, which were all of porcelain, glittered with a thousand gold lamps; the loveliest flowers, with the merriest tinkling bells, were placed in the passages; there was a running to and fro, which made all the bells ring, so that one could not hear his own words.

In the midst of the grand hall where the Emperor sat, a golden perch was erected, on which the nightingale was to sit. The whole court was present, and the little kitchen-maid received permission to stand behind the door, for she had now actually the rank and title of "Maid of the Kitchen". All were dressed out in their finest clothes; and all eyes were fixed upon the little grey bird, to whom the Emperor nodded as a signal for her to begin.

And the nightingale sang so sweetly, that tears came into the Emperor's eyes, tears rolled down his cheeks; and the nightingale sang more sweetly still, and touched the hearts of all who heard her; and the Emperor was so merry, that he said, "The nightingale should have my golden slippers, and wear them round her neck." But the nightingale thanked him, and said she was already sufficiently rewarded.

"I have seen tears in the Emperor's eyes, that is the greatest reward I can have. The tears of an Emperor have a particular value. Heaven knows I am sufficiently rewarded."

And then she sang again with her sweet, lovely voice.

... the nightingale sang so sweetly, that tears came into the Emperor's eyes

"It is the most amiable coquetry ever known," said the ladies present; and they put water into their mouths, and tried to move their throats as she did, when they spoke; they thought to become nightingales also. Indeed even the footmen and chamber-maids declared that they were quite contented; which was a great thing to say, for of all people they are the most difficult to satisfy. Yes, indeed, the nightingale's success was complete. She was now to remain at court to have her own cage; with permission to fly out twice in the day and once in the night. Twelve attendants were allotted her who were to hold a silken band, fastened round her foot: and they kept good hold. There was no pleasure in excursions made in this manner.

All the city was talking of the wonderful bird; and when two persons met, one would say only "night," and the other "gale," and then they sighed, and understood each other perfectly; indeed eleven of the children of the citizens were named after the nightingale, but none of them had her tones in their throats.

One day a large parcel arrived for the Emperor, on which was written "Nightingale".

"Here we have another new book about our far-famed bird," said the Emperor. But it was not a book; it was a little piece of mechanism, lying in a box; an artificial nightingale, which was intended to look like the living one, but was covered over with diamonds, rubies, and sapphires. When this artificial bird had been wound up, it could sing one of the tunes that the real nightingale sang; and its tail all glittering with silver and gold, went up and down all the time. A little band was fastened round its neck, on which was written, "The nightingale of the Emperor of China is poor compared with the nightingale of the Emperor of Japan."

"That is famous!" said every one; and he who had brought the bird, obtained the title of "Chief Imperial Nightingale Bringer". "Now they shall sing together; we will have a duet."

And so they must sing together; but it did not suceed, for the real nightingale sang in her own way, and the artificial bird produced its tones by wheels. "It is not his fault," said the artist, "he keeps exact time and quite according to method."

So the artificial bird must now sing alone; he was quite as successful as the real nightingale; and then he was so much prettier to look at; his plumage sparkled like jewels.

Three and thirty times he sang one and the same tune, and yet he was not weary; every one would willingly have heard him again; however, the Emperor now wished the real nightingale should sing something—but where was she? No one had remarked that she had flown out of the open window; flown away to her own green wood.

"What is the meaning of this?" said the Emperor; and all the courtiers abused the nightingale, and called her a most ungrateful creature. "We have the best bird at all events," said they, and for the four-and-thirtieth time they heard the same tune, but still they did not quite know it, because it was so difficult. The artist praised the bird inordinately; indeed he declared it was superior to the real nightingale, not only in its exterior, all sparkling with diamonds, but also intrinsically.

"For see, my noble lords, His Imperial Majesty especially, with the real nightingale, one could never reckon on what was coming; but everything is settled with the artificial bird; he will sing in this one way, and no other: this can be proved, he can be taken to pieces, and the works can be shown, where the wheels lie, how they move, and how one follows from another."

"That is just what I think," said everybody; and the artist received permission to show the bird to the people on the following Sunday. "They too should hear him sing," the Emperor said. So they heard him, and were as well pleased as if they had all been drinking tea; for it is tea that makes Chinese merry, and they all said "Oh!" and raised their forefingers, and nodded their heads.

But the fisherman, who had heard the real nightingale, said, "It sounds very pretty, almost like the real bird; but yet there is some-

He had obtained the rank and title of "High Imperial Dessert Singer"

thing wanting; I do not know what."

The real nightingale was, however, banished from the empire.

The artificial bird had his place on a silken cushion, close to the Emperor's bed; all the presents he received, gold and precious stones, lay around him; he had obtained the rank and title of "High Imperial Dessert Singer" and, therefore, his place was number one on the left side; for the Emperor thought that the side where the heart was situated must be the most honourable, and the heart is situated on the left side of an Emperor, as well as with other folks.

And the artist wrote five-and-twenty volumes about the artificial bird, with the longest and most difficult words that are to be found in the Chinese language. So, of course, all said they had read and understood them, otherwise they would have been stupid, and perhaps would have been flogged.

Thus it went on for a year. The Emperor, the court, and all the Chinese knew every note of the artificial bird's song by heart; but that was the very reason they enjoyed it so much, they could now sing with him. The little boys in the street sang "zizizi, cluck, cluck, cluck!" and the Emperor himself sang too—yes, indeed, that was charming!

But one evening, when the bird was in full voice, and the Emperor lay in bed, and listened, there was suddenly a noise, "bang," inside the bird, then something sprang "fur-r-r-r," all the wheels were running about, and the music stopped.

The Emperor jumped quickly out of bed, and had his chief physician called; but of what use could he be? Then a clockmaker was fetched, and at last, after a great deal of discussion and consultation, the bird was in some measure put to rights again; but the clockmaker said, he must be spared much singing, for the pegs were almost worn out, and it was impossible to renew them, at least so that the music should be correct.

There was great lamentation, for now the artificial bird was allowed to sing only once a year, and even then there were difficulties; however, the artist made a short speech full of his favourite long words, and said the bird was as good as ever; so then, of course, it was as good as ever.

When five years were passed away, a great affliction visited the whole empire, for in their hearts the people thought highly of their Emperor; and now he was ill, and it was reported that he could not live. A new Emperor had already been chosen, and the people stood in the street, outside the palace, and asked the Cavalier how the Emperor was?

"Pish!" said he, and shook his head.

Cold and pale lay the Emperor in his magnificent bed; all the court believed him to be already dead, and every one had hastened away to greet the new Emperor; the men ran out for a little gossip on the subject, and the maids were having a grand coffee party.

The floors of all the rooms and passages were covered with cloth, in order that not a step should be heard—it was everywhere so still! so still! But the Emperor was not yet dead; stiff and pale he lay in his splendid bed, with the long velvet curtains and heavy gold tassels. A window was opened above, and the moon shone down on the Emperor and the artificial bird.

The poor Emperor could scarcely breathe; it appeared to him as though something was sitting on his chest; he opened his eyes, and saw that it was Death, who had put on the Emperor's crown, and with one hand held the golden scimitar, with the other the splendid imperial banner; whilst, from under the folds of the thick velvet hangings, the strangest-looking heads were seen peering forth; some with an expression absolutely hideous, and others with an extremely gentle and lovely aspect: they were the bad and good deeds of the Emperor, which were now all fixing their eyes upon him, whilst Death sat on his heart.

"Dost thou know this?" they whispered one after another. "Dost thou remember that?" And they began reproaching him in such a manner that the sweat broke out upon his forehead.

"I have never known anything like it," said the Emperor. "Music, music, the great Chinese drum!" cried he, "let me not hear what they are saying."

They went on, however; and Death, quite in the Chinese fashion, nodded his head to every word.

"Music, music!" cried the Emperor. "Then dear little artificial bird! sing, I pray thee, sing!—I have given thee gold and precious stones, I have even hung my golden slippers round thy neck—sing, I pray thee, sing!"

But the bird was silent; there was no one there to wind him up, and he could not sing without this. Death continued to stare at the Emperor with his great hollow eyes! and everywhere it was still, fearfully still!

All at once the sweetest song was heard from the window; it was the little living nightingale who was sitting on a branch outside—she had heard of her Emperor's severe illness, and was come to sing to him of comfort and hope. As she sang, the spectral forms became paler and paler, the blood flowed more and more quickly through the Emperor's feeble members, and even Death listened and said, "Go on, little nightingale, go on."

"Wilt thou give me the splendid gold scimitar? Wilt thou give me the gay banner, and the Emperor's crown?"

And Death gave up all these treasures for a song; and the nightingale sang on: she sang of the quiet churchyard, where white roses blossom, where the lilac sends forth its fragrance, and the fresh grass is bedewed with the tears of the sorrowing friends of the departed. Then Death was seized with a longing after his garden, and like a cold white shadow, flew out at the window.

"Thanks, thanks," said the Emperor, "thou heavenly little bird, I know thee well. I have banished thee from my realm, and thou hast sung away those evil faces from my bed, and death from my heart; how shall I reward thee?"

"Thou hast already rewarded me," said the nightingale, "I have seen tears in thine eyes, as when I sang to thee for the first time: those I shall never forget, they are jewels which do so much good to a minstrel's heart! but sleep now, and wake fresh and healthy; I will sing thee to sleep."

And she sang—and the Emperor fell into a sweet sleep. Oh, how soft and kindly was that sleep!

The sun shone in at the window when he awoke, strong and healthy. Not one of his servants had returned, for they all believed him dead; but the nightingale still sat and sang.

"Thou shalt always stay with me," said the Emperor, "thou shalt only sing when it pleases thee, and the artificial bird I will break into a thousand pieces."

"Do not so," said the nightingale; "truly he has done what he could; take care of him. I cannot stay in the palace; but let me come when I like: I will sit on the branches close to the window, in the evening, and sing to thee, that thou mayest become happy and thoughtful. I will sing to thee of the joyful and the sorrowing, I will sing to thee of all that is good or bad, which is concealed from thee. The little minstrel flies afar to the fisherman's hut, to the peasant's cottage, to all who are far distant from thee and thy court. I love thy heart more thy crown, and yet the crown has an odour of something holy about it. I will come, I will sing. But thou must promise me one thing."

"Everything," said the Emperor. And now he stood in his imperial splendour, which he had put on himself, and held the scimitar so heavy with gold to his heart.—"One thing I beg of thee: let no one know that thou hast a little bird, who tells thee everything, then all will go on well." And the nightingale flew away.

The attendants came in to look at their dead Emperor—lo! there they stood—and the Emperor said, "Good-morning."

THE SWINEHERD

THERE was once a poor Prince, who had a kingdom; his kingdom was very small, but still quite large enough to marry upon; and he wished to marry.

It was certainly rather cool of him to say to the Emperor's daughter, "Will you have me?" But so he did; for his name was renowned far and wide; and there were a hundred princesses who would have answered "Yes!" and "Thank you kindly." We shall see what this Princess said.

Listen!

It happened that where the Prince's father lay buried, there grew a rose-tree—a most beautiful rose-tree, which blossomed only once in every five years, and even then bore only one flower, but that *was* a rose! It smelt so sweet, that all cares and sorrows were forgotten by him who inhaled its fragrance.

And furthermore, the Prince had a nightingale, who could sing in such a manner that it seemed as though all sweet melodies dwelt in her little throat. So the Princess was to have the rose, and the nightingale; and they were accordingly put into large silver caskets, and sent to her.

The Emperor had them brought into a large hall, where the Princess was playing at "Visiting," with the ladies of the court; and when she saw the caskets with the presents, she clapped her hands for joy.

"Ah, if it were but a little pussy-cat!" said she—but the rose-tree with its beautiful rose came to view.

"Oh, how prettily it is made!" said all the court ladies.

"It is more than pretty," said the Emperor, "it is charming!"

But the Princess touched it, and was almost ready to cry.

"Fie, papa!" said she, "it is not made at all, it is natural!"

"Let us see what is in the other casket, before we get into a bad humour," said the Emperor. So the nightingale came forth, and sang so delightfully that no one could say anything ill-humoured of her.

"*Superbe! charmante!*" exclaimed the ladies; for they all used to chatter French, each one worse than her neighbour.

"How much the bird reminds me of the musical box that belonged to our blessed Empress," said an old knight. "Oh yes! these are the same tones, the same execution."

"Yes! yes!" said the Emperor, and he wept like a child at the remembrance.

"I will still hope that it is not a real bird," said the Princess.

"Yes, it is a real bird," said those who had brought it.

"Well, then, let the bird fly," said the Princess; and she positively refused to see the Prince.

However, he was not to be discouraged; he daubed his face over brown and black; pulled his cap over his ears, and knocked at the door.

"Good day to my lord the Emperor!" said he. "Can I have employment at the palace?"

"Why, yes," said the Emperor, "I want some one to take care of the pigs, for we have a great many of them."

So the Prince was appointed "Imperial Swineherd". He had a dirty little room close by the pig-sty; and there he sat the whole day, and worked. By the evening he had made a pretty little kitchen-pot. Little bells were hung all around it; and when the pot was boiling, these bells tinkled in the most charming manner, and played the old melody:

> "*Ach! du lieber Augustin,*
> *Alles ist weg, weg, weg!*"

But what was still more curious, whoever held his finger in the smoke of the kitchen-pot, immediately smelt all the dishes that were cooking on every hearth in the city—this, you see, was something quite different from the rose.

Now the Princess happened to walk that way; and when she heard

1 "*Ah! dear Augustine!*
All is gone, gone, gone!"

the tune she stood quite still, and seemed pleased; for she could play "Lieber Augustin"; it was the only piece she knew; and she played it with one finger.

"Why, there is my piece," said the Princess, "that swineherd must certainly have been well educated! go in and ask him the price of the instrument."

So one of the court-ladies must run in; however, she drew on wooden slippers first.

"What will you take for the kitchen-pot?" said the lady.

"I will have ten kisses from the Princess," said the swineherd.

"Yes, indeed!" said the lady.

"I cannot sell it for less," rejoined the swineherd.

"He is an impudent fellow!" said the Princess, and she walked on —but when she had gone a little way, the bells tinkled so prettily—

> *"Ach! du lieber Augustin,*
> *Alles ist weg, weg, weg!"*[1]

"Stay," said the Princess. "Ask him if he will have ten kisses from the ladies of my court."

"No, thank you!" said the swineherd, "ten kisses from the Princess, or I keep the kitchen-pot myself."

"That must not be either!" said the Princess; "but do you all stand before me that no one may see us."

And the court-ladies placed themselves in front of her, and spread out their dresses—the swineherd got ten kisses, and the Princess—the kitchen-pot.

That was delightful! the pot was boiling the whole evening, and the whole of the following day. They knew perfectly well what was cooking at every fire throughout the city, from the chamberlain's to the cobbler's: the court-ladies danced, and clapped their hands.

"We know who has soup, and who has pancakes for dinner to-day; who has cutlets, and who has eggs. How interesting!"

"Yes, but keep my secret, for I am an Emperor's daughter."

55

...the swineherd got ten kisses

The swineherd—that is to say, the Prince, for no one knew that he was other than an ill-favoured swineherd—let not a day pass without working at something; he at last constructed a rattle, which, when it was swung round, played all the waltzes and jig-tunes which have ever been heard since the creation of the world.

"Ah, that is *superbe!*" said the Princess when she passed by. "I have never heard prettier compositions! Go in and ask him the price of the instrument; but mind, he shall have no more kisses!"

"He will have a hundred kisses from the Princess!" said the lady who had been to ask.

"I think he is not in his right senses!" said the Princess, and walked on; but when she had gone a little way, she stopped again. "One must encourage art," said she. "I am the Emperor's daughter. Tell him he shall, as on yesterday, have ten kisses from me, and may take the rest from the ladies of the court."

"Oh!—but we should not like that at all!" said they. "What are you muttering?" asked the Princess; "if I can kiss him, surely you can! Remember that you owe everything to me." So the ladies were obliged to go to him again.

"A hundred kisses from the Princess!" said he, "or else let every one keep his own."

"Stand round!" said she; and all the ladies stood round her whilst the kissing was going on.

"What can be the reason for such a crowd close by the pig-sty?" said the Emperor, who happened just then to step out on the balcony. He rubbed his eyes and put on his spectacles. "They are the ladies of the court; I must go down and see what they are about!" So he pulled up his slippers at the heel, for he had trodden them down.

As soon as he had got into the courtyard, he moved very softly, and the ladies were so much engrossed with counting the kisses that all might go on fairly that they did not perceive the Emperor. He rose on his tip-toes.

"What is all this?" said he, when he saw what was going on, and he boxed the Princess's ears with his slipper, just as the swineherd was taking the eighty-sixth kiss.

"March out!" said the Emperor, for he was very angry; and both Princess and swineherd were thrust out of the city.

The Princess now stood and wept, the swineherd scolded, and the rain poured down.

"Alas! unhappy creature that I am!" said the Princess. "If I had but married the handsome young Prince! Ah! how unfortunate I am!"

And the swineherd went behind a tree, washed the black and brown colour from his face, threw off his dirty clothes, and stepped forth in his princely robes; he looked so noble that the Princess could not help bowing before him.

"I am come to despise thee," said he. "Thou wouldst not have an honourable prince! thou couldst not prize the rose and the nightingale, but thou wast ready to kiss the swineherd for the sake of a trumpery plaything. Thou art rightly served."

He then went back to his own little kingdom, and shut the door of his palace in her face. Now she might well sing

"Ach! du lieber Augustin,
Alles ist weg, weg, weg!"

THE EMPEROR'S NEW CLOTHES

MANY years ago, there was an Emperor, who was so excessively fond of new clothes that he spent all his money on dress. He did not trouble himself in the least about his soldiers; nor did he care to go either to the theatre or the chase, except for the opportunities then afforded him for displaying his new cothes. He had a different suit for each hour of the day; and as of any other king or emperor, one is accustomed to say, "He is sitting in council," it was always said of him. "The Emperor is sitting in his wardrobe."

Time passed away merrily in the large town which was his capital; strangers arrived every day at the court. One day, two rogues, calling themselves weavers, made their appearance. They gave out that they knew how to weave stuffs of the most beautiful colours and elaborate patterns, the clothes manufactured from which should have the wonderful property of remaining invisible to every one who was unfit for the office he held, or who was extraordinarily simple in character.

"These must indeed be splendid clothes!" thought the Emperor. "Had I such a suit, I might, at once, find out what men in my realms are unfit for their office, and also be able to distinguish the wise from the foolish! This stuff must be woven for me immediately." And he caused large sums of money to be given to both the weavers, in order that they might begin their work directly.

So the two pretended weavers set up two looms, and affected to work very busily, though in reality they did nothing at all. They asked for the most delicate silk and the purest gold thread; put both into their own knapsacks; and then continued their pretended work at the empty looms until late at night.

"I should like to know how the weavers are getting on with my cloth," said the Emperor to himself, after some little time had elapsed; he was, however, rather embarrassed, when he remembered that a simpleton, or one unfit for his office, would be unable to see the manufacture. "To be sure," he thought, "I have nothing to risk in my own person; but yet, I would prefer sending somebody else, to bring me intelligence about the weavers, and their work, before I trouble myself in the affair." All the people throughout the city had heard of the wonderful property the cloth was to possess; and all were anxious to learn how wise, or how ignorant, their neighbours might prove to be.

"I will send my faithful old minister to the weavers," said the

Emperor at last, after same deliberation, "he will be best able to see how the cloth looks; for he is a man of sense, and no one can be more suitable for his office than he is."

So the faithful old minister went into the hall, where the knaves were working with all their might at their empty looms. "What can be the meaning of this?" thought the old man, opening his eyes very wide. "I cannot discover the least bit of thread on the looms!" However, he did not express his thoughts aloud.

The impostors requested him very courteously to be so good as to come nearer their looms; and then asked him whether the design pleased him, and whether the colours were not very beautiful; at the same time pointing to the empty frames. The poor old minister looked and looked; he could not discover anything on the looms, for a very good reason, viz.: there was nothing there. "What!" thought he again, "is it possible that I am a simpleton? I have never thought so myself; and no one must know it now if I am so. Can it be that I am unfit for my office? No, that must not be said either. I will never confess that I could not see the stuff."

"Well, Sir Minister!" said one of the knaves, still pretending to work, "you do not say whether the stuff pleases you."

"Oh, it is excellent!" replied the old minister, looking at the loom through his spectacles. "This pattern, and the colours—yes, I will tell the Emperor without delay how very beautiful I think them."

"We shall be much obliged to you," said the impostors, and then they named the different colours and described the pattern of the pretended stuff. The old minister listened attentively to their words, in order that he might repeat them to the Emperor; and then the knaves asked for more silk and gold, saying that it was necessary to complete what they had begun. However, they put all that was given them into their knapsacks; and continued to work with as much apparent diligence as before at their empty looms.

The Emperor now sent another officer of his court to see how the men were getting on, and to ascertain whether the cloth would soon be ready. It was just the same with this gentleman as with the minister; he surveyed the looms on all sides, but could see nothing at all but the empty frames.

"Does not the stuff appear as beautiful to you as it did to my lord the minister?" asked the impostors of the Emperor's second ambassador; at the same time making the same gestures as before, and talking of the design and colours which were not there.

"I certainly am not stupid!" thought the messenger. "It must be that I am not fit for my good, profitable office! That is very odd; however, no one shall know anything about it." And accordingly he praised the stuff he could not see, and declared that he was delighted with both colours and patterns. "Indeed, please your Imperial Majesty," said he to his sovereign, when he returned, "the cloth which the weavers are preparing is extraordinarily magnificent."

The whole city was talking of the splendid cloth which the Emperor had ordered to be woven at his own expense.

And now the Emperor himself wished to see the costly manufacture whilst it was still on the loom. Accompanied by a select number of officers of the court, among whom were the two honest men who had already admired the cloth, he went to the crafty impostors, who as soon as they were aware of the Emperor's approach, went on working more diligently than ever; although they still did not pass a single thread through the looms.

"Is not the work absolutely magnificent?" said the two officers of the crown, already mentioned. "If your Majesty will only be pleased to look at it! what a splendid design! what glorious colours!" and, at the same time, they pointed to the empty frames; for they imagined that every one else could see this exquisite piece of workmanship.

"How is this?" said the Emperor to himself. "I can see nothing! this is indeed a terrible affair! Am I a simpleton, or am I unfit to be an Emperor? that would be the worst thing that could happen—oh! the cloth is charming," said he, aloud. "It has my complete approbation." And he smiled most graciously, and looked closely at the empty looms; for on no account would he say that he could not see what two of the officers of his court had praised so much. All his retinue now strained their eyes, hoping to discover something on the looms, but they could see no more than the others; nevertheless, they all exclaimed, "Oh, how beautiful!" and advised his Majesty to have some clothes made from this splendid material, for the approaching procession. "Magnificent! charming! excellent!" resounded on all sides; and every one was uncommonly gay. The Emperor shared in the general satisfaction; and presented the impostors with the riband of an order of knighthood, to be worn in their button-holes, and the title of "Gentlemen Weavers".

The rogues sat up the whole of the night before the day on which the procession was to take place, and had sixteen lights burning, so that every one might see how anxious they were to finish the Emperor's new suit. They pretended to roll the cloth off the looms: cut the air with their scissors; and sewed with needles without any thread in them. "See!" cried they at last, "the Emperor's new clothes are ready!"

And now the Emperor, with all the grandees of his court, came to the weavers; and the rogues raised their arms, as if in the act of holding something up, saying, "Here are your Majesty's trousers! here is the scarf! here is the mantle! The whole suit is as light as a cobweb; one might fancy one has nothing at all on, when dressed in it; that, hoewever, is the great virtue of this delicate cloth."

"Yes, indeed!" said all the courtiers, although not one of them could see anything of this exquisite manufacture.

"If your Imperial Majesty will be graciously pleased to take off your clothes, we will fit on the new suit, in front of the looking-glass."

The Emperor was accordingly undressed, and the rogues pretended to array him in his new suit; the Emperor turning round, from side to side, before the looking-glass.

"How splendid his Majesty looks in his new clothes! and how well they fit!" every one cried out. "What a design! what colours! these are indeed royal robes!"

"The canopy which is to be borne over your Majesty in the procession is waiting," announced the chief master of the ceremonies.

"I am quite ready," answered the Emperor. "Do my new clothes fit well?" asked he, turning himself round again before the looking-glass, in order that he might appear to be examining his handsome suit.

The lords of the bed-chamber, who were to carry his Majesty's train, felt about on the ground, as if they were lifting up the ends of the mantle; and pretended to be carrying something; for they would by no means betray anything like simplicity or unfitness for their office.

So now the Emperor walked under his high canopy in the midst of the procession, through the streets of his capital; and all the people standing by, and those at the windows, cried out, "Oh! how beautiful are our Emperor's new clothes! what a magnificent train there is to the mantle; and how gracefully the scarf hangs!" In short, no one would allow that he could not see these much-admired clothes; because, in doing so, he would have declared himself either a simpleton or unfit for his office. Certainly, none of the Emperor's various suits had ever made so great an impression as these invisible ones.

"But the Emperor has nothing at all on!" said a little child.

"Listen to the voice of innocence!" exclaimed his father; and what the child had said was whispered from one to another.

"But he has nothing at all on!" at last cried out all the people. The Emperor was vexed, for he knew that the people were right; but he thought the procession must go on now: And the lords of the bed-chamber took greater pains than ever, to appear holding up a train, although, in reality, there was no train to hold.

Far away in the deep forest there once grew a pretty Fir-Tree: the situation was delightful, the sun shone full upon him, the breeze played freely around him, and in the neighbourhood grew many companion fir-trees, some older, some younger. But the little Fir-Tree was not happy: he was always longing to be tall; he thought not of the warm sun and the fresh air; he cared not for the merry, prattling peasant children who came to the forest to look for strawberries and raspberries. Except indeed, sometimes, when after having filled their pitchers, or threaded the bright berries on a straw, they would sit down near the little Fir-Tree, and say, "What a pretty little tree this is;" and then the Fir-Tree would feel very much vexed.

Year by year he grew, a long green shoot sent he forth every year; for you may always tell how many years a fir-tree has lived by counting the number of joints in its stem.

"Oh, that I was as tall as the others are," sighed the little Tree; "then I should spread out my branches so far, and my crown should look out over the wide world around! The birds would build their nests among my branches, and when the wind blew I should bend my head so grandly, just as the others do!" He had no pleasure in the sunshine, in the song of the birds, or in the red clouds that sailed over him every morning and evening.

In the winter-time when the ground was covered with the white glistening snow, there was a hare that would come continually scampering about, and jumping right over the little Tree's head—and that was most provoking! However, two winters passed away, and by the third the Tree was so tall that the hare was obliged to run round it. "Oh! to grow, to grow, to become tall and old, that is the only thing in the world worth living for;" so thought the Tree.

The wood-cutters came in the autumn and felled some among the largest of the trees; this happened every year, and our young fir, who was by this time a tolerable height, shuddered when he saw those

...the tree was so tall that the hare was obliged to run round it

grand, magnificent trees fall with a tremendous crash crackling to the earth; their boughs were then all cut off; terribly naked and lanky and long did the stem look after this—they could hardly be recognised. They were laid one upon another in waggons, and horses drew them away, far, far away from the forest.

Where could they be going? What might be their fortunes?

So next spring, when the swallows and the storks had returned from abroad, the Tree asked them, saying, "Know you not whither they are taken? Have you not met them?"

The swallows knew nothing about the matter, but the stork looked thoughtful for a moment, then he nodded his head, and said, "Yes, I believe I have seen them! As I was flying from Egypt to this place I met several ships; those ships had splendid masts. I have little doubt that they were the trees that you speak of; they smelled like fir-wood. I may congratulate you, for they sailed gloriously, quite gloriously!"

"Oh, that I too were tall enough to sail upon the sea! Tell me what it is, this sea! and what it looks like."

"Thank you, it would take too long, a great deal!" said the stork, and away he stalked.

"Rejoice in thy youth!" said the sunbeams; "rejoice in thy luxuriant youth, in the fresh life that is within thee!"

And the wind kissed the Tree, and the dew wept tears over him, but the Fir-Tree understood them not.

When Christmas approached, many quite young trees were felled, trees which were some of them not so tall or of just the same height as the young restless Fir-Tree who was always longing to be away; these young trees were chosen from the most beautiful, their branches were not cut off, they were laid in a waggon, and horses drew them away, far, far away from the forest.

"Where are they going?" asked the Fir-Tree. "They are not larger than I am, indeed one of them was much less; why do they keep all their branches? Where can they be gone?"

"We know! we know!" twittered the sparrows. "We peeped in

through the windows of the town below! We know where they are gone. Oh, you cannot think what honour and glory they receive! We looked through the window-panes and saw them planted in a warm room, and decked out with such beautiful things, gilded apples, sweetmeats, playthings, and hundreds of bright candles!"

"And then?" asked the Fir-Tree, trembling in every bough; "and then? What happened then?"

"Oh! we saw no more. That was beautiful, beautiful beyond compare!"

"Is this glorious lot destined to be mine?" cried the Fir-Tree with delight. "This is far better than sailing over the sea. How I long for the time. Oh, that Christmas were come! I am now tall and full of branches, like the others which last year were carried away. Oh, that I were even now in the waggon! that I were in the warm room, honoured and adorned! and then—yes, then, something still better must happen, else why should they take the trouble to decorate me? It must be that something still greater, still more splendid, must happen—but what? Oh, I suffer, I suffer with longing! I know not what it is that I feel."

"Rejoice in our love," said the air and the sunshine. "Rejoice in thy youth and thy freedom!"

But rejoice he never would. He grew and grew, in winter as in summer; he stood there clothed in green, dark green foliage; the people that saw him said, "That is a beautiful tree!" and, next Christmas, he was the first that was felled. The axe struck sharply through the wood, the Tree fell to the earth with a heavy groan; he suffered an agony, a faintness that he had never expected; he quite forgot to think of his good fortune, he felt such sorrow at being compelled to leave his home, the place whence he had sprung; he knew that he should never see again those dear old comrades, or the little bushes and flowers that had flourished under his shadow, perhaps not even the birds. Neither did he find the journey by any means pleasant.

The Tree first came to himself when, in the courtyard to which he was first taken with the other trees, he heard a man say, "This is a splendid one, the very thing we want!"

Then came two smartly-dressed servants, and carried the Fir-Tree into a large and handsome saloon. Pictures hung on the walls, and on the mantelpiece stood large Chinese vases with lions on the lids; there were rocking-chairs, silken sofas, tables covered with picture-books, and toys that had cost a hundred times a hundred dollars, at least, so said the childen. And the Fir-Tree was planted in a large cask filled with sand; but no one could know that it was a cask, for it was hung with green cloth and placed upon a carpet woven of many gay colours. Oh, how the Tree trembled! What was to happen next? A young lady, assisted by the servants, now began to adorn him. Upon some branches they hung little nets cut out of coloured paper, every net filled with sugar-plums; from others gilded apples and walnuts were suspended, looking just as if they had grown there, and more than a hundred little wax tapers, red, blue, and white, were placed here and there among the boughs. Dolls that looked almost like men and women—the Tree had never seen such things before—seemed dancing to and fro among the leaves, and highest, on the summit, was fastened a large star of gold tinsel; this was indeed splendid, splendid beyond compare.

"This evening," they said, "this evening it will be lighted up."

"Would that it were evening," thought the Tree. "Would that the lights were kindled, for then—what will happen then? Will the trees come out of the forest to see me? Will the sparrows fly here and look in through the window-panes? Shall I stand here adorned both winter and summer?"

He thought much of it; he thought till he had barkache with long-ing, and barkaches with trees are as bad as headaches with us.

The candles were lighted—oh, what a blaze of splendour! The Tree trembled in all its branches so that one of them caught fire. "Oh dear!" cried the young lady, and it was extinguished in great haste.

68

So the Tree dared not tremble again; he was so fearful of losing something of his splendour, he felt almost bewildered in the midst of all this glory and brightness. And now, all of a sudden, both folding-doors were flung open, and a troop of children rushed in as if they had a mind to jump over him; the older people followed more quietly; the little ones stood quite silent, but only for a moment. Then their jubilee burst forth afresh, they shouted till the walls re-echoed, they danced round the Tree, one present after another was torn down.

"What are they doing?" throught the Tree; "what will happen now?" And the candles burnt down to the branches, so they were ex-tinguished—and the children were given leave to plunder the Tree. Oh! they rushed upon him in such riot that the boughs all crackled; had not his summit been festooned with the gold star to the ceiling he would have been overturned.

The children danced and played about with their beautiful play-things; no one thought any more of the Tree except the old nurse, who came and peeped among the boughs, but it was only to see whether perchance a fig or an apple had not been left among them.

"A story! a story!" cried the children, pulling a short, thick man towards the Tree. He sat down, saying, "It is pleasant to sit under the shade of green boughs; besides, the tree may benefit by hearing my story. But I shall only tell you one. Would you like to hear about Ivedy Avedy, or about Humpty Dumpty, who fell downstairs, and yet came to the throne and won the Princess?"

"Ivedy Avedy!" cried some! "Humpty Dumpty!" cried others; there was a famous uproar. The Fir-Tree alone was silent, thinking to himself, "Ought I to make a noise as they do? or ought I to do nothing at all?" for he most certainly was one of the company, and had done all that had been required of him.

And the short, thick man told the story of Humpty Dumpty, who fell downstairs and yet came to the throne and won the Princess. And the children clapped their hands and called out for another;

they wanted to hear the story of Ivedy Avedy also, but they did not get it. The Fir-Tree stood meanwhile quite silent and thoughtful, the birds in the forest had never related antyhing like this. "Humpty Dumpty fell downstairs, and yet was raised to the throne and won the Princess! Yes, yes, strange things come to pass in the world!" thought the Fir-Tree, who believed it must all be true, because such a pleasant man had related it. "Ah, ah! who knows but I may fall downstairs and win a Princess!" And he rejoiced in the expectation of being next day again decked out with candles and playthings, gold and fruit. "To-morrow I will not tremble," thought he. "I will rejoice in my magnificence. To-morrow I shall again hear the story of Humpty Dumpty, and perhaps that about Ivedy Avedy likewise." And the Tree mused thereupon all night.

In the morning the maids came in.

"Now begins my state anew!" thought the Tree. But they dragged him out of the room, up the stairs, and into an attic chamber, and there thrust him into a dark corner where not a ray of light could penetrate. "What can be the meaning of this?" thought the Tree. "What am I to do here? What shall I hear in this place?" And he leant against the wall, and thought, and thought. And plenty of time he had for thinking it over, for day after day, and night after night passed away, and yet no one ever came into the room. At last somebody did come in, but it was only to push into the corner some old trunks. The Tree was now entirely hidden from sight and apparently entirely forgotten.

"It is now winter," thought the Tree. "The ground is hard and covered with snow; they cannot plant me now, so I am to stay here in shelter till the spring. Men are so clever and prudent! I only wish it were not so dark and so dreadfully lonely; not even a little hare! Oh, how pleasant it was in the forest, when the snow lay on the ground and the hare scampered about, yes, even when he jumped over my head, though I did not like it then. It is so terribly lonely here."

"Squeak! squeak!" cried a little mouse, just then gliding forward. Another followed; they snuffed about the Fir-Tree, and then slipped in and out among the branches.

"It is horribly cold!" said the little mice. "Otherwise it is very comfortable here. Don't you think so, you old Fir-Tree?"

"I am not old," said the Fir-Tree; "there are many who are much older than I am."

"How came you here?" asked the mice, "and what do you know?" They were most uncommonly curious. "Tell us about the most delightful place on earth? Have you ever been there? Have you been into the storeroom, where cheeses lie on the shelves, and bacon hangs from the ceiling; where one can dance over tallow-candles; where one goes in thin and comes out fat?"

"I know nothing about that," said the Tree; "but I know the forest, where the sun shines and where the birds sing!" and then he spoke of his youth and its pleasures. The little mice had never heard anything like it before; they listened so attentively and said, "Well, to be sure! how much you have seen! how happy you have been!"

"Happy!" repeated the Fir-Tree, in surprise, and he thought a moment over all that he had been saying. "Yes, on the whole those were pleasant times!" He then told them about the Christmas Eve when he had been decked out with cakes and candles.

"Oh!" cried the little mice, "how happy you have been, you old Fir-Tree!"

"I am not old at all!" returned the Fir; "it is only this winter that I have left the forest. I am just in the prime of life!"

"How well you can talk!" said the little mice, and the next night they came again and brought with them four other little mice, who wanted also to hear the Tree's history; and the more the Tree spoke of his youth in the forest, the more vividly he remembered it, and said, "Yes, those were pleasant times! but they may come again, they may come again! Humpty Dumpty fell downstairs, and yet for all that he won the Princess; perhaps I, too, may win a princess!" And then the Fir-Tree thought of a pretty little delicate birch-tree that grew in the forest—a real princess, a very lovely princess was she to the Fir-Tree.

"Who is this Humpty Dumpty?" asked the little mice. Whereupon he related the tale; he could remember every word of it perfectly: and the little mice were ready to jump to the top of the Tree for joy. The night following several more mice came, and on Sunday came also two rats; they, however, declared that the story was not at all amusing, which much vexed the little mice, who, after hearing their opinion, could not like it so well either.

"Do you know only that one story?" asked the rats.

"Only that one!" answered the Tree; "I heard it on the happiest evening of my life, though I did not then know how happy I was."

"It is a miserable story; do you know none about pork and tallow? No storeroom story?"

"No," said the Tree.

"Well, then, we have heard enough of it!" returned the rats, and they went their ways.

The little mice, too, never came again. The Tree sighed, "It was pleasant when they sat round me, those busy little mice, listening to my words. Now that, too, is all past! However, I shall have pleasure in remembering it, when I am taken from this place."

But when would that be? One morning, people came and routed out the lumber-room; the trunks were taken away, the Tree, too, was dragged out of the corner; they threw him carelessly on the floor, but one of the servants picked him up and carried him downstairs. Once more he beheld the light of day. "Now life begins again!" thought the Tree. He felt the fresh air, the warm sunbeams—he was out in the court. All happened so quickly that the Tree quite forgot to look at himself—there was so much to look at all around. The court joined a garden, everything was so fresh and blooming, the roses clustered so bright and so fragrant round the trellis-work, the lime-trees were in full blossom, and the swallows flew backwards and forwards, twittering, "Quirri-virri, vit, my beloved is come!" But it was not the Fir-Tree whom they meant.

"I shall live! I shall live!" He was filled with delightful hope; he tried to spread out his branches, but alas! they were all dried up and yellow. He was thrown down upon a heap of weeds and nettles. The star of gold tinsel that had been left fixed on his crown now sparkled brightly in the sunshine. Some merry children were playing in the court, the same who at Christmas-time had danced round the Tree. One of the youngest now perceived the gold star, and ran to tear it off.

"Look at it, still fastened to the ugly old Christmas Tree!" cried he, trampling upon the boughs till they broke under his boots.

And the Tree looked on all the flowers of the garden now blooming in the freshness of their beauty; he looked upon himself, and he wished from his heart that he had been left to wither alone in the dark corner of the lumber-room: he called to mind his happy forest-life, the merry Christmas Eve, and the little mice who had listened so eagerly when he related the story of Humpty Dumpty.

"Past, all past!" said the poor Tree. "Had I but been happy, as I might have been! Past, all past!"

And the servant came and broke the tree into small pieces, heaped them up and set fire to them. And the Tree groaned deeply, and every groan sounded like a little shot. The children all ran up to the place and jumped about in front of the blaze, looking into it and crying, "Piff! piff!" But at each of those heavy groans, the Fir-Tree thought of a bright summer's day, or a starry winter's night in the forest, of Christmas Eve, or of Humpty Dumpty, the only story that he knew and could relate. And at last the Tree was burned.

The boys played about in the court; on the bosom of the youngest sparkled the gold star that the Tree had worn on the happiest evening of his life; but that was past, and the story also, past, past, for all stories must come to an end, some time or other.

THE SNOW QUEEN
Part One
Which treats of the mirror and its fragments

LISTEN! We are beginning our story! When we arrive at the end of it we shall, it is to be hoped, know more than we do now. There was once a magician! a wicked magician!! a most wicked magician!!! Great was his delight at having constructed a mirror possessing this peculiarity, viz.:—that everything good and beautiful, when reflected in it, shrank up almost to nothing, whilst those things that were ugly and useless were magnified, and made to appear ten times worse than before. The loveliest landscapes reflected in this mirror looked like boiled spinach; and the handsomest persons appeared odious, or as if standing upon their heads, their features being so distorted that their friends could never have recognised them. Moreover, if one of them had a freckle, he might be sure that it would seem to spread over the nose and mouth; and if a good or pious thought glanced across his mind, a wrinkle was seen in the mirror. All this the magician thought highly entertaining, and he chuckled with delight at his own clever invention. Those who frequented the school of magic where he taught, spread abroad the fame of this wonderful mirror, and declared that by its means the world and its inhabitants might be seen now for the first time as they really were. They carried the mirror from place to place, till at last there was no country nor person that had not been misrepresented in it. Its admirers now must needs fly up to the sky with it, to see if they could not carry on their sport even there. But the higher they flew the more wrinkled did the mirror become; they could scarcely hold it together. They flew on and on, higher and higher, till at last the mirror trembled so fearfully that it escaped from their hands, and fell to the earth, breaking into millions, billions, and trillions of pieces. And then it caused far greater unhappiness than before, for fragments of it, scarcely as large as a grain of sand, would be flying about in the air, and sometimes get into people's eyes, causing them to view everything the wrong way, or to have eyes only for what was perverted and corrupt; each little fragment having retained the peculiar properties of the entire mirror. Some people were so unfortunate as to receive a little splinter into their hearts—that was terrible! The heart became cold and hard, like a lump of ice. Some pieces were large enough to be used as window panes, but it was of no use to look at one's friends through such panes as those. Other fragments were made into spectacles, and then what trouble people had with setting and re-setting them!

The wicked magician was greatly amused with all this, and he laughed till his sides ached.

There are still some little splinters of this mischievous mirror flying about in the air. We shall hear more about them very soon.

Part Two
A little boy and a little girl

IN a large town, where there are so many houses and inhabitants that there is not room enough for all the people to possess a little garden of their own, and therefore many are obliged to content themselves with keeping a few plants in pots, there dwelt two poor children, whose garden was somewhat larger than a flowerpot. They were not brother and sister, but they loved each other as much as if they had been, and their parents lived in two attics exactly opposite. The roof of one neighbour's house nearly joined the other, the gutter ran along between, and there was in each roof a little window, so that you could stride across the gutter from one window to the other. The parents of each child had a large wooden box in which grew herbs for kitchen use, and they had placed these boxes upon the gutter, so near that they almost touched each other. A beautiful little rose-tree grew in each pot, scarlet runners entwined their long shoots over the windows, and, uniting with the branches of the rose-trees, formed a flowery arch across the street. The boxes were very high, and the children knew that they might not climb over them, but they often obtained leave to sit on their little stools, under the rose-trees, and thus they passed many a delightful hour.

But when winter came there was an end to these pleasures.

The windows were often quite frozen over, and then they heated halfpence on the stove, held the warm copper against the frozen pane, and thus made a little round peep-hole, behind which would sparkle a bright gentle eye, one from each window.

The little boy was called Kay, the little girl's name was Gerda. In summer time they could get out of the window and jump over to each other; but in winter there were stairs to run down, and stairs to run up, and sometimes the wind roared, and the snow fell outdoors.

"Those are the white bees swarming there!" said the old grandmother.

"Have they a Queen bee?" asked the little boy, for he knew that the real bees have one.

"They have," said the grandmother. "She flies yonder where they swarm so thickly; she is the largest of them, and never remains upon the earth, but flies up again into the black cloud. Sometimes on a winter's night she flies through the streets of the town, and breathes with her frosty breath upon the windows, and then they are covered with strange and beautiful forms, like trees and flowers."

"Yes, I have seen them!" said both the children—they knew that this was true.

"Can the Snow Queen come in here?" asked the little girl.

"If she does come in," said the boy, "I will put her on the warm stove and then she will melt."

And the grandmother stroked his hair and told him some stories.

That same evening, after little Kay had gone home, and was half undressed, he crept upon the chair by the window and peeped through the little round hole. Just then a few snowflakes fell outside, and one, the largest of them, remained lying on the edge of one of the flower-pots. The snowflake appeared larger and larger, and at last took the form of a lady dressed in the finest white crêpe, her attire being composed of millions of starlike particles. She was exquisitely fair and delicate, but entirely of ice, glittering, dazzling ice; her eyes gleamed like two bright stars, but there was no rest or repose in them. She nodded at the window, and beckoned with her hand. The little boy was frightened and jumped down from the chair; he then fancied he saw a large bird fly past the window.

There was a clear frost next day, and soon afterwards came spring; the trees and flowers budded, the swallows built their nests, the windows were opened, and the little children sat once more in their little garden upon the gutter that ran along the roof of the houses.

The roses blossomed beautifully that summer, and the little girl had learned a hymn in which there was something about roses; it reminded her of her own. So she sang it to the little boy, and he sang it with her.

> "Our roses bloom and fade away,
> Our Infant Lord abides alway;
> May we be blessed His face to see,
> And ever little children be!"

And the little ones held each other by the hand, kissed the roses, and looked up into the blue sky, talking away all the time. What glorious summer days were those! how delightful it was to sit under those rose-trees which seemed as if they never intended to leave off blossoming! One day Kay and Gerda were sitting looking at their picture-book full of birds and animals, when suddenly—the clock on the old church tower was just striking five—Kay exclaimed, "Oh, dear! what was that shooting pain in my heart? And now again, something has certainly got into my eye!"

The little girl turned and looked at him. He winked his eyes; no, there was nothing to be seen.

"I believe it is gone," said he; but gone it was not. It was one

She was exquisitely fair and delicate

of those glass splinters from the Magic Mirror, the wicked glass which made everything great and good reflected in it to appear little and hateful, and which magnified everything ugly and mean. Poor Kay had also received a splinter in his heart; it would now become hard and cold like a lump of ice. He felt the pain no longer, but the splinter was there.

"Why do you cry?" asked he; "you look so ugly when you cry! There is nothing the matter with me. Fie!" exclaimed he again, "this rose has an insect in it, and just look at this! after all, they are ugly roses! and it is an ugly box they grow in!" Then he kicked the box, and tore off the roses.

"O Kay, what are you doing?" cried the little girl, but when he saw how it grieved her, he tore off another rose, and jumped down through his own window, away from his once dear little Gerda.

Ever afterwards when she brought forward the picture-book, he called it a baby's book, and when her grandmother told stories, he interrupted her with a "but," and sometimes, whenever he could manage it, he would get behind her, put on her spectacles, and speak just as she did; he did this in a very droll manner, and so people laughed at him. Very soon he could mimic everybody in the street. All that was singular and awkward about them could Kay imitate, and his neighbours said, "What a remarkable head that boy has!" But no, it was the glass splinter which had fallen into his eye, the glass splinter which had pierced into his heart—it was these which made him regardless whose feelings he wounded, and even made him tease the Gerda who loved him so fondly.

His games were now quite different from what they used to be, they were so rational! One winter's day when it was snowing, he came out with a large burning-glass in his hand, and, holding up the skirts of his blue coat, let the snowflakes fall upon them. "Now look through the glass, Gerda!" said he, returning to the house. Every snowflake seemed much larger, and resembled a splendid flower, or a star with ten points; they were quite beautiful. "See, how curious!"

said Kay, "these are far more interesting than real flowers, there is not a single blemish in them; they would be quite perfect if only they did not melt."

Soon after this Kay came in again, with thick gloves on his hands, and his sledge slung across his back. He called out to Gerda, "I have got leave to drive on the great square where the other boys play!" and away he went.

The boldest boys in the square used to fasten their sledges firmly to the waggons of the country people, and thus drive a good way along with them; this they thought particularly pleasant. Whilst they were in the midst of their play a large sledge, painted white, passed by; in it sat a person wrapped in a rough white fur, and wearing a rough white cap. When the sledge had driven twice round the square, Kay bound to it his little sledge, and was carried on with it. On they went, faster and faster, into the next street. The person who drove the large sledge turned round and nodded kindly to Kay, just as if they had been old acquaintances, and every time Kay was going to loose his little sledge, turned and nodded again, as if to signify that he must stay. So Kay sat still, and they passed through the gates of the town. Then the snow began to fall so thickly that the little boy could not see his own hand, but he was still carried on. He tried hastily to unloose the cords and free himself from the large sledge, but it was of no use; his little carriage could not be unfastened, and glided on swift as the wind. Then he cried out as loud as he could, but no one heard him; the snow fell and the sledge flew; every now and then it made a spring as if driving over hedges and ditches. He was very much frightened; he would have repeated "Our Father," but he could remember nothing but the multiplication table.

The snowflakes seemed larger and larger; at last they looked like great white birds. All at once they fell aside, the large sledge stopped, and the person who drove it arose from the seat. He saw that the cap and coat were entirely of snow; that it was a lady, tall and slender, and dazzlingly white—it was the Snow Queen!

They flew over woods and over lakes, over sea and over land

"We have driven fast!" said she, "but no one likes to be frozen; creep under my bear-skin," and she seated him in the sledge by her side, and spread her cloak around him—he felt as if he were sinking into a drift of snow.

"Are you still cold?" asked she, and then she kissed his brow. Oh! her kiss was colder than ice. It went to his heart, although that was half frozen already; he thought he should die. It was, however, only for a moment; directly afterwards he was quite well, and no longer felt the intense cold around.

"My sledge! do not forget my sledge!"—he thought first of that— it was fastened to one of the white birds, which flew behind with it on his back. The Snow Queen kissed Kay again, and he entirely forgot little Gerda, her grandmother, and all at home.

"Now you must have no more kisses!" said she, "else I should kiss thee to death."

Kay looked at her, she was so beautiful; a more intelligent, more lovely countenance, he could not imagine; she no longer appeared to him ice, cold ice, as at the time when she sat outside the window and beckoned to him; in his eyes she was perfect; he felt no fear. He told her how well he could reckon in his head, even fractions; that he knew the number of square miles of every country, and the number of the inhabitants contained in different towns. She smiled, and then it occurred to him that, after all, he did not yet know so very much. He looked up into the wide, wide space, and she flew with him high up into the black cloud while the storm was raging; it seemed now to Kay as though singing songs of olden time.

They flew over woods and over lakes, over sea and over land; beneath them the cold wind whistled, the wolves howled, the snow glittered, and the black crow flew cawing over the plain, whilst above them shone the moon, so clear and tranquil.

Thus did Kay spend the long, long winter night; all day he slept at the feet of the Snow Queen.

Part Three
The enchanted flower garden

But how fared it with little Gerda when Kay never returned? Where could he be? No one knew, no one could give any account of him. The boys said that they had seen him fasten his sledge to another larger and very handsome one which had driven into the street, and thence through the gates of the town. No one knew where he was, and many were the tears that were shed; little Gerda wept much and long, for the boys said he must be dead, he must have been drowned in the river that flowed not far from the town. Oh, how long and dismal the winter days were now! At last came the spring, with its warm sunshine.

"Alas, Kay is dead and gone," said little Gerda.

"That I do not believe," said the sunshine.

"He is dead and gone," said she to the swallows.

"That we do not believe," returned they, and at last little Gerda herself did not believe it.

"I will put on my new red shoes," said she one morning, "those which Kay has never seen, and then I will go down to the river and ask after him."

It was quite early. She kissed her old grandmother, who was still sleeping, put on her red shoes, and went alone through the gates of the town towards the river.

"Is it true," said she, "that thou hast taken my little playfellow away? I will give thee my red shoes if thou wilt restore him to me!"

And the wavelets of the river flowed towards her in a manner which she fancied was unusual; she fancied that they intended to accept her offer, so she took off her red shoes—though she prized them more than anything else she possessed—and threw them into the stream; but they fell near the shore, and the little waves bore them back to her, as though they would not take from her what she most prized, as they had not got little Kay. However, she thought she had not thrown the shoes far enough, so she stepped into a little boat which lay among the reeds by the shore, and, standing at the farthest end of it, threw them from thence into the water. The boat was not fastened, and her movements in it caused it to glide away from the shore. She saw this, and hastened to get out, but, by the time she reached the other end of the boat, it was more than a yard distant from the land; she could not escape, and the boat glided on.

Little Gerda was much frightened and began to cry, but no one besides the sparrows heard her, and they could not carry her back to the land; however, they flew along the banks, and sang, as if to comfort her, "Here we are, here we are!" The boat followed the stream. Little Gerda sat in it quite still; her red shoes floated behind her, but they could not overtake the boat, which glided along faster than they did.

Beautiful were the shores of that river; lovely flowers, stately old trees, and bright green hills dotted with sheep and cows, were seen in abundance, but not a single human being.

"Perhaps the river may bear me to my dear Kay," thought Gerda, and then she became more cheerful, and amused herself for hours with looking at the lovely country around her. At last she glided past a large cherry garden, wherein stood a little cottage with thatched roof and curious red and blue windows; two wooden soldiers stood at the door, who presented arms when they saw the little vessel approach.

Gerda called to them, thinking they were alive; but they, naturally enough, made no answer. She came close up to them, for the stream drifted the boat to the land.

Gerda called still louder, whereupon an old lady came out of the house, supporting herself on a crutch; she wore a large hat, with most beautiful flowers painted on it.

"Thou poor little child!" said the old woman, "the mighty flowing river has indeed borne thee a long, long way," and she walked right into the water, seized the boat with her crutch, drew it to land, and took out the little girl.

Gerda was glad to be on dry land again, although she was a little afraid of the strange old lady.

"Come and tell me who thou art, and how thou camest hither," said she.

And Gerda told her all, and the old lady shook her head, and said, "Hem! hem!" And when Gerda asked if she had seen little Kay, the lady said that he had not arrived there yet, but that he would be sure to come soon, and that in the meantime Gerda must not be sad; that she might stay with her, might eat her cherries, and look at her flowers, which were prettier than any picture-book, and could each tell her a story.

She then took Gerda by the hand; they went together into the cottage, and the old lady shut the door. The windows were very high and their panes of different coloured glass, red, blue, and yellow, so that when the bright daylight streamed through them, various and beautiful were the hues reflected upon the room. Upon a table in the centre was placed a plate of very fine cherries, and of these Gerda was allowed to eat as many as she liked. And whilst she was eating them, the old dame combed her hair with a golden comb, and the bright flaxen ringlets fell on each side of her pretty, gentle face, which looked as round and as fresh as a rose.

"I have long wished for such a dear little girl," said the old lady. "We shall see if we cannot live very happily together." And, as she combed little Gerda's hair, the child thought less and less of her foster-brother Kay, for the old lady was an enchantress. She did not, however, practise magic for the sake of mischief, but merely for her own amusement. And now she wished very much to keep little Gerda, to live with her; so, fearing that if Gerda saw her roses, she would be reminded of her own flowers and of little Kay, and that then she might run away, she went out into the garden, and extended her crutch over all her rose-bushes, upon which, although they were full of leaves and blossoms, they immediately sank into the black earth, and no one would have guessed that such plants had ever grown there.

Then she led Gerda into this flower-garden. Oh, how beautiful and how fragrant it was! Flowers of all seasons and all climes grew there in fullness of beauty—certainly no picture-book could be compared with it. Gerda bounded with delight, and played among the flowers till the sun set behind the tall cherry-trees; after which a pretty little bed, with crimson silk cushions, stuffed with blue violet leaves, was prepared for her, and here she slept as sweetly and had such dreams as a queen might have on her bridal eve.

The next day she again played among the flowers in the warm sunshine, and many more days were spent in the same manner. Gerda knew every flower in the garden, but, numerous as they were, it seemed to her that one was wanting, she could not tell which. She was sitting one day, looking at her hostess's hat, which had flowers painted on it, and, behold, the loveliest among them was a rose! The old lady had entirely forgotten the painted rose on her hat, when she made the real roses to disappear from her garden and sink into the ground. This is often the case when things are done hastily.

"What," cried Gerda, "are there no roses in the garden?" And she ran from one bed to another, sought and sought again, but no rose was to be found. She sat down and wept, and it so chanced that her tears fell on a spot where a rose-tree had formerly stood, and as soon as her warm tears had moistened the earth, the bush shot up anew, as fresh and as blooming as it was before it had sunk into the ground; and Gerda threw her arms around it, kissed the blossoms, and immediately recalled to memory the beautiful roses at home, and her little playfellow Kay. "Oh, how could I stay here so long!" exclaimed the little maiden. "I left my home to seek for Kay. Do you know where he is?" she asked of the roses; "think you that he is dead?"

"Dead he is not," said the roses. "We have been down in the

earth; the dead are there, but not Kay."

"I thank you," said little Gerda, and she went to the other flowers, bent low over their cups, and asked, "Know you not where little Kay is?"

But every flower stood in the sunshine dreaming its own little tale. They related their stories to Gerda, but none of them knew anything of Kay.

"What says the tiger-lily?"

"Listen to the drums beating, boom! boom! They have but two notes, always boom! boom! Listen to the dirge the women are singing! Listen to the chorus of priests! Enveloped in her long red robes stands the Hindoo wife on the funeral pile, the flames blaze around her and her dead husband, but the Hindoo wife thinks not of the dead. She thinks only of the living, and the anguish which consumes her spirit is keener than the fire which will soon reduce her body to ashes. Can the flame of the heart expire amid the flames of the funeral pile?"

"I do not understand that at all!" said little Gerda.

"That is my tale!" said the tiger-lily.

"What says the convolvulus?"

"Hanging over a narrow mountain causeway, behold an ancient, baronial castle. Thick evergreens grow amongst the time-stained walls, their leafy branches entwine about the balcony, and there stands a beautiful maiden; she bends over the balustrades and fixes her eyes with eager expectation on the road winding beneath. The rose hangs not fresher and lovelier on its stem than she; the apple-blossom which the wind threatens every moment to tear from its branch is not more fragile and trembling. Listen to the rustling of her rich silken robe! Listen to her half-whispered words, 'He comes not!'"

"Is it Kay you mean?" asked little Gerda.

"I do but tell you my tale—my dream," replied the convolvulus.

"What says the little snowdrop?"

"Between two trees hangs a swing. Two pretty little maidens, their dress as white as snow, and long green ribands fluttering from their hats, sit and swing themselves in it. Their brother stands up in the swing, he has thrown his arms round the ropes to keep himself steady, for in one hand he holds a little cup, in the other a pipe made of clay; he is blowing soap bubbles. The swing moves and the bubbles fly upwards with bright, ever-changing colours; the last hovers on the edge of the pipe, and moves with the wind. The swing is still in motion, and the little black dog, almost as light as the soap bubbles, rises on his hind feet and tries to get into the swing also; away goes the swing, the dog falls, is out of temper, and barks; he is laughed at, and the bubbles burst. A swinging board, a frothy, fleeting image is my song."

"What you describe may all be very pretty, but you speak so mournfully, and there is nothing about Kay."

"What say the hyacinths?"

"There were three fair sisters, transparent and delicate they were; the kirtle of the one was red, that of the second blue, of the third pure white; hand in hand they danced in the moonlight beside the quiet lake; they were not fairies, but daughters of men. Sweet was the fragrance when the maidens vanished into the wood; the fragrance grew stronger; three biers, whereon lay the fair sisters, glided out from the depths of the wood, and floated upon the lake; the glow-worms flew shining around like little hovering lamps. Sleep the dancing maidens, or are they dead? The odour from the flowers tells us they are corpses, the evening bells peal out their dirge."

"You make me quite sad," said little Gerda. "Your fragrance is so strong I cannot help thinking of the dead maidens. Alas! and is little Kay dead? The roses have been under the earth, and they say no!"

"Ding dong! ding dong!" rang the hyacinth bells. "We toll not for little Kay, we know him not! We do but sing our own song."

And Gerda went to the buttercup, which shone so yellow and so brightly from among her smooth green leaves.

"Thou art like a little bright sun," said Gerda; "tell me, if thou canst, where I may find my playfellow."

And the buttercup glittered so brightly, and looked at Gerda. What song could the buttercup sing? Neither was hers about Kay. "One bright spring morning, the sun shone warmly upon a little court-yard, the bright beams streamed down the white walls of a neighbouring house, and close by grew the first yellow flower of spring, glittering like gold in the warm sunshine. An old grand-mother sat without in her arm-chair; her grand-daughter, a pretty, lowly maiden, had just returned home from a short visit, she kissed her grandmother; there was gold, pure gold, in that loving kiss:

"Gold was the flower!
Gold the fresh, bright, morning hour!"

"That is my little story," said the buttercup.

"My poor old grandmother!" sighed Gerda; "yes, she must be wishing for me, just as she wished for little Kay. But I shall soon go home again, and take Kay with me. It is of no use to ask the flowers about him; they only know their own song, they can give me no information." And she folded her little frock round her, that she might run the faster; but, in jumping over the narcissus, it caught her foot, as if wishing to stop her, so she turned and looked at the tall yellow flower.

"Have you any news to give me?" She bent over the narcissus, waiting for an answer.

And what said the narcissus?

"I can look at myself!—I can see myself! Oh, how sweet is my fragrance! Up in the little attic-chamber stands a little dancer. She rests sometimes on one leg, sometimes on two. She has trampled the whole world under her feet; she is nothing but an illusion. She pours water from a tea-pot upon a piece of cloth she holds in her hand—it is her bodice; cleanliness is a fine thing! Her white dress hangs on the hook, that has also been washed by the water from the tea-pot, and dried on the roof of the house. She puts it on, and wraps a saffron-coloured handkerchief round her neck; it makes the dress look all the whiter. With one leg extended, there she stands, as though on a stalk. I can look at myself!—I see myself!"

"I don't care if you do!" said Gerda. "You need not have told me that!" and away she ran to the end of the garden.

The gate was closed, but she pressed upon the rusty lock till it broke. The gate sprang open, and little Gerda, with bare feet, ran out into the wide world. Three times she looked back, there was no one following her; she ran till she could run no longer, and then sat down to rest upon a large stone.

Casting a glance around, she saw that the summer was past, that it was now late in the autumn. Of course, she had not remarked this in the enchanted garden, where there were sunshine and flowers all the year round.

"How long I must have stayed there!" said little Gerda. "So it is now autumn! Well then, there is no time to lose!" and she rose to pursue her way.

Oh how sore and weary were her little feet! and all around looked so cold and barren. The long willow-leaves had already turned yellow, and the dew trickled down from them like water. The leaves fell off the trees, one by one; the sloe alone bore fruit, and its berries were so sharp and bitter! Cold, and grey, and sad seemed the world to her that day.

Part Four
The prince and the princess

GERDA was again obliged to stop and take rest. Suddenly a large raven hopped upon the snow in front of her, saying, "Caw!—Caw!— Good-day!—Good-day!" He sat for some time on the withered branch of a tree just opposite, eyeing the little maiden, and wagging his head, and he now came forward to make acquaintance and to ask her whither she was going all alone. That word "alone" Gerda understood right well—she felt how sad a meaning it had. She told the raven the history of her life and fortunes, and asked if he had seen Kay.

And the raven nodded his head, half doubtfully, and said, "That is possible—possible."

"Do you think so?" exclaimed the little girl, and she kissed the raven so vehemently that it is a wonder she did not squeeze him to death.

"More moderately!—moderately!" said the raven. "I think I know. I think it may be little Kay; but he has certainly forsaken thee for the princess."

"Dwells he with a princess?" asked Gerda.

"Listen to me," said the raven, "but it is so difficult to speak your language! Do you understand Ravenish? If so, I can tell you much better."

"No! I have never learned Ravenish," said Gerda, "but my grand-mother knew it, and Pye-language also. Oh, how I wish I had learned it!"

"Never mind," said the raven, "I will relate my story in the best manner I can, though bad will be the best;" and he told all he knew.

"In the kingdom wherein we are now sitting there dwells a princess, a most uncommonly clever princess. All the newspapers in the world has she read, and forgotten them again, so clever is she. It is not long since she ascended the throne, which I have heard is not quite so agreeable a situation as one would fancy; and immediately after she began to sing a new song, the burden of which was this, 'Why should I not marry me?' 'There is some sense in this song!' said she, and she determined she would marry, but at the same time declared that the man whom she would choose must be able to answer sensibly whenever people spoke to him, and must be good for something else besides merely looking grand and stately. The ladies of the court were then all drummed together, in order to be informed of her intentions, whereupon they were highly delighted, and one exclaimed, 'That is just what I wish;' and another, that she had lately been thinking of the very same thing. Believe me." continued the raven, "every word I say is true, for I have a tame beloved who hops at pleasure about the palace, and she has told me all this."

Of course the "beloved" was also a raven, for birds of a feather flock together.

"Proclamations, adorned with borders of hearts, were immediately issued, wherein, after enumerating the style and titles of the princess, it was set forth that every well-favoured youth was free to go to the palace and converse with the princess, and that whoever should speak in such wise as showed that he felt himself at home, there would be the one the princess would choose for her husband.

"Yes, indeed," continued the raven, "you may believe me; all this is as true as that I sit here. The people all crowded to the palace; there was famous pressing and squeezing; but it was all of no use, either the first or the second day; the young men could speak well enough while they were outside the palace gates, but when they entered, and saw the royal guard in silver uniform, and the lackeys on the staircase in gold, and the spacious saloon, all lighted up, they were quite confounded. They stood before the throne where the princess sat, and when she spoke to them, they could only repeat the last word she had uttered, which, you know, it was not particularly interesting for her to hear over again. It was just as though they had been struck dumb the moment they entered the palace, for as soon as they got out, they could talk fast enough. There was a regular procession constantly moving from the gates of the town to the gates of the palace. I was there, and saw it with my own eyes," said the raven. "They grew both hungry and thirsty whilst waiting at the palace, but no one could get even so much as a glass of water; to be sure, some of them, wiser than the rest, had brought with them slices of bread and butter, but none would give any to his neighbour, for he thought to himself 'Let him look hungry, and then the princess will be sure not to choose him.'"

"But Kay, little Kay, when did he come?" asked Gerda; "was he among the crowd?"

"Presently, presently; we have just come to him. On the third day arrived a youth with neither horse nor carriage; gaily he marched up to the palace; his eyes sparkled like yours; he had long beautiful hair, but was very meanly clad."

"That was Kay!" exclaimed Gerda. "Oh then I have found him," and she clapped her hands with delight.

"He carried a knapsack on his back," said the raven.

"No, not a knapsack," said Gerda, "a sledge, for he had a sledge with him when he left home."

"It is possible," rejoined the raven, "I did not look very closely; but this I heard from my beloved, that when he entered the palace gates and saw the royal guard in silver, and the lackeys in gold upon the staircase, he did not seem in the least confused, but nodded pleasantly and said to them, 'It must be very tedious standing out here, I prefer going in.' The halls glistened with light, cabinet councillors and excellencies were walking about bare-footed and carrying golden keys—it was just a place to make a man solemn and silent—and the youth's boots creaked horribly, yet he was not at all afraid."

"That most certainly was Kay!" said Gerda; "I know he had new boots; I have heard them creak in my grandmother's room."

"Indeed they did creak," said the raven; "but merrily went he up to the princess, who was sitting upon a pearl as large as a spinning-wheel, whilst all the ladies of the court, with the maids of honour and their handmaidens, ranged in order, stood on one side, and all the gentlemen in waiting, with their gentlemen, and their gentlemen's gentlemen, who also kept pages, stood ranged in order on the other side, and the nearer they were to the door the prouder they looked. The gentlemen's gentlemen's page, who always wears slippers, one dare hardly look at, so proudly he stands at the door."

"That must be dreadful!" said little Gerda. "And has Kay really won the princess?"

"Had I not been a raven I should have won her myself, notwithstanding my being betrothed. The young man spoke as well as I speak when I converse in Ravenish; that I have heard from my tame beloved. He was handsome and lively—'He did not come to woo her,' he said, 'he had only come to hear the wisdom of the princess,' and he liked her much, and she liked him in return."

"Yes, to be sure, that was Kay," said Gerda; "he was so clever, he could reckon in his head, even fractions! Oh, will you not take me into the palace?"

"Ah! that is easily said," replied the raven, "but how is it to be done? I will talk it over with my tame beloved; she will advise us what to do, for I must tell you that such a little girl as you are will never gain permission to enter publicly."

"Yes, I shall!" cried Gerda. "When Kay knows that I am here, he will immediately come out and fetch me."

"Wait for me at the trellis yonder," said the raven. He wagged his head and away he flew.

The raven did not return till late in the evening. "Caw, caw," said he. "My tame beloved greets you kindly, and sends you a piece of bread which she took from the kitchen; there is plenty of bread there, and you must certainly be hungry. It is not possible for you to enter the palace, for you have bare feet; the royal guard in silver uniform, and the lackeys in gold, would never permit it; but do not weep, thou shalt go there. My beloved knows a little back staircase leading to the sleeping apartments, and she knows also where to find the key."

And they went into the garden, down the grand avenue, where the leaves dropped upon them as they passed along, and, when the lights in the palace one by one had all been extinguished, the raven took

Gerda to a back-door which stood half open. Oh, how Gerda's heart beat with fear and expectation! It was just as though she was about to do something wrong, although she only wanted to know whether Kay was really there—yes, it must be he, she remembered so well his bright eyes and long hair. She would see if his smile were the same as it used to be when they sat together under the rose-trees. He would be so glad to see her, to hear how far she had come for his sake, how all at home mourned his absence. Her heart trembled with fear and joy.

They went up the staircase. A small lamp placed on a cabinet gave a glimmering light; on the floor stood the tame raven, who first turned her head on all sides, and then looked at Gerda, who made her curtsey, as her grandmother had taught her.

"My betrothed has told me much about you, my good young maiden," said the tame raven; "your adventures, too, are extremely interesting! If you will take the lamp, I will show you the way. We are going straight on, we shall not meet any one now."

"It seems me as if some one were behind us," said Gerda; and in fact there was a rushing sound as of something passing; strange-looking shadows flitted rapidly along the wall, horses with long, slender legs and fluttering manes, huntsmen, knights, and ladies.

"These are only Dreams!" said the raven; "they come to amuse the great personages here at night; you will have a better opportunity of looking at them when you are in bed. I hope that when you arrive at honours and dignities you will show a grateful heart."

"Do not talk of that!" said the wood-raven.

They now entered the first saloon; its walls were covered with rose-coloured satin, embroidered with gold flowers. The Dreams rustled past them, but with such rapidity that Gerda could not see them. The apartments through which they passed vied with each other in splendour, and at last they reached the sleeping-hall. In the centre of this room stood a pillar of gold resembling the stem of a large palm-tree, whose leaves of glass, costly glass, formed the ceiling, and depending from the tree, hung near the door, on thick golden stalks, two beds in the form of lilies—the one was white, wherein reposed the princess, the other was red, and here must Gerda seek her playfellow, Kay. She bent aside one of the red leaves and saw a brown neck. Oh, it must be Kay! She called him by his name aloud, held the lamp close to him, the Dreams again rushed by—he awoke, turned his head, and behold! it was not Kay.

The prince resembled him only about the throat; he was, however, young and handsome; and the princess looked out from the white lily petals, and asked what was the matter. Then little Gerda wept and told her whole story, and what the ravens had done for her. "Poor child!" said the prince and princess; and they praised the ravens, and said they were not at all angry with them. Such liberties must never be taken again in their palace, but this time they should be rewarded.

"Would you like to fly away free to the woods?" asked the princess, addressing the ravens, "or to have the appointment secured to you as Court-Ravens, with the perquisites belonging to the kitchen, such as crumbs and leavings?"

And both the ravens bowed low and chose the appointment at Court, for they thought of old age, and said it would be so comfortable to be well provided for in their declining years. Then the prince arose and made Gerda sleep in his bed; and she folded her little hands, thinking, "How kind both men and animals are to me!" She closed her eyes and slept soundly and sweetly, and all the Dreams flitted about her, they looked like angels from heaven, and seemed to be drawing a sledge whereon Kay sat and nodded to her; but this was only fancy, for as soon as she awoke all the beautiful visions had vanished.

The next day she was dressed from head to foot in silk and velvet. She was invited to stay at the palace and enjoy all sorts of diversions, but she begged only for a little carriage and a horse, and a pair of little boots,—to go again into the wide world to seek Kay.

And they gave her the boots and a muff besides; she was dressed so prettily. And as soon as she was ready there drove up to the door a new carriage of pure gold with the arms of the prince and princess glittering upon it like a star, the coachman, the footman, and outriders all wearing gold crowns. The prince and princess themselves helped her into the carriage and wished her success. The woodraven, who was now married, accompanied her the first three miles; he sat by her side, for riding backwards was a thing he could not bear; the other raven stood at the door flapping her wings; she did not go with them on account of a headache she had felt ever since she had received her appointment, in consequence of eating too much. The carriage was well provided with sugar-plums, fruit, and gingerbread nuts.

"Farewell! farewell!" cried the prince and princess. Little Gerda wept, and the raven wept out of sympathy; but his farewell was a far sorer trial; he flew up to the branch of a tree and flapped his black wings at the carriage till it was out of sight.

Part Five
The little robber maiden

THEY drove through the dark, dark forest; the carriage shone like a torch. Unfortunately its brightness attracted the eyes of the robbers who dwelt in the forest-shades; they could not bear it.

"That is gold! gold!" cried they. Forward they rushed, seized the horses, stabbed the outriders, coachman, and footmen to death, and dragged little Gerda out of the carriage.

"She is plump, she is pretty, she has been fed on nutkernels," said the old robber-wife, who had a long, bristly beard, and eyebrows hanging like bushes over her eyes. "She is like a little fat lamb, and how smartly she is dressed!" and she drew out her bright dagger, glittering most terribly.

She put her arm round Gerda's waist

"Oh, oh!" cried the woman, for at the very moment she had lifted her dagger to stab Gerda, her own wild and wilful daughter jumped upon her back and bit her ear violently. "You naughty child!" said the mother.

"She shall play with me," said the little robber-maiden, "she shall give me her muff and her pretty frock, and sleep with me in my bed!" And then she bit her mother again, till the robber-wife sprang up and shrieked with pain, whilst the robbers all laughed, saying, "Look at her playing with her young one!"

"I will get into the carriage," said the little robber-maiden, and so spoiled and wayward was she that she always had her own way, and she and Gerda sat together in the carriage, and drove over stock and stone farther and farther into the wood. The little robber-maiden was about as tall as Gerda, but much stronger; she had broad shoulders, and a very dark skin; her eyes were quite black, and had an expression almost melancholy. She put her arm round Gerda's waist, and said, "She shall not kill thee so long as I love thee! Art thou not a princess?"

"No!" said Gerda; and then she told her all that had happened to her, and how much she loved little Kay.

The robber-maiden looked earnestly in her face, shook her head, and said, "She shall not kill thee even if I do quarrel with thee; then, indeed, I would rather do it myself!" And she dried Gerda's tears, and put both her hands into the pretty muff that was so soft and warm.

The carriage at last stopped in the middle of the court-yard of the robbers, castle. This castle was half-ruined; crows and ravens flew out of the openings, and some fearfully large bulldogs, looking as if they could devour a man in a moment, jumped round the carriage; they did not bark, for that was forbidden.

The maidens entered a large, smoky hall, where a trememdous fire was blazing on the stone floor; the smoke rose up to the ceiling, seeking a way of escape, for there was no chimney; a large cauldron full of soup was boiling over the fire, whilst hares and rabbits were roasting on the spit.

"Thou shalt sleep with me and my little pets to-night!" said the robber-maiden. Then they had some food, and afterwards went to the corner wherein lay straw and a piece of carpet. Nearly a hundred pigeons were perched on staves and laths around them; they seemed to be asleep, but were startled when the little maidens approached.

"These all belong to me," said Gerda's companion, and seizing hold of one of the nearest, she held the poor bird by the feet and swung it. "Kiss it," said she, flapping it into Gerda's face. "The rabble from the wood sit up there," continued she, pointing to a number of laths fastened across a hole in the wall; "those are wood-pigeons, they would fly away if I did not keep them shut up. And here is my old favourite!" She pulled forward by the horn a reindeer who wore a bright copper ring round his neck, by which he was fastened to a large stone. "We are obliged to chain him up, or he would run away from us; every evening I tickle his neck with my sharp dagger; it makes him fear so much!" and the robber-maiden drew out a long dagger from a gap in the wall, and passed it over the reindeer's throat; the poor animal struggled and kicked, but the girl laughed, and then she pulled Gerda into bed with her.

"Will you keep the dagger in your hand whilst you sleep?" asked Gerda, looking timidly at the dangerous plaything.

"I always sleep with my dagger by my side," replied the little robber-maiden, "one never knows what may happen. But now tell me all over again what you told me before about Kay, and the reason of your coming into the wide world all by yourself."

And Gerda again related her history, and the wood-pigeons im-prisoned above listened, but the others were fast asleep. The little robber-maiden threw one arm round Gerda's neck, and holding the dagger with the other, was also soon asleep; one could hear her heavy breathing, but Gerda could not close her eyes throughout the night—she knew not what would become of her, whether she would even be suffered to live. The robbers sat round the fire drinking and singing. Oh, it was a dreadful night for the poor little girl!

Then spoke the wood-pigeons, "Coo, coo, coo! we have seen little Kay. A white fowl carried his sledge, he himself was in the Snow Queen's chariot, which passed through the wood whilst we sat in our nest. She breathed upon us young ones as she passed, and all died of her breath excepting us two,—coo, coo, coo!"

"What are you saying?" cried Gerda. "Where was the Snow Queen going? Do you know anything about it?"

"She travels most likely to Lapland, where ice and snow abide all the year round. Ask the reindeer bound to the rope there."

"Yes, ice and snow are there all through the year, it is a glorious land!" said the reindeer. "There, free and happy, one can roam through the wide, sparkling valleys! There the Snow Queen has her summer-tent; her strong castle is very far off, near the North Pole, on the island called Spitsbergen."

"O Kay, dear Kay!" sighed Gerda.

"You must lie still," said the robber-maiden, "or I will thrust my dagger into your side."

When morning came Gerda repeated to her what the wood-pigeons had said, and the little robber-maiden looked grave for a moment, then nodded her head, saying, "No matter! no matter! Do you know where Lapland is?" asked she of the reindeer.

"Who should know but I?" returned the animal, his eyes kindling. "There was I born and bred, there how often have I bounded over the wild icy plains!"

"Listen to me!" said the robber-maiden to Gerda. "You see all our men are gone, my mother is still here and will remain, but towards noon she will drink a little out of the great flask, and after that she will sleep—then I will do something for you!" And so saying she jumped out of bed, sprung upon her mother, pulled her by the beard, and said, "My own dear mam, good morning!" and the mother caressed her so roughly that she was red and blue all over;

however, it was from pure love for her daughter.

When her mother was fast asleep, the robber-maiden went up to the reindeer, and said, "I should have great pleasure in stroking you a few more times with my sharp dagger, for then you look so droll; but never mind, I will unloose your chain and help you to escape, on condition that you run as fast as you can to Lapland, and take this little girl to the castle of the Snow Queen, where her playfellow is. You must have heard her story, for she speaks loud enough, and you know well how to listen."

The reindeer bounded with joy, and the robber-maiden lifted Gerda on his back, taking the precaution to bind her on firmly, as well as to give her a little cushion to sit on. "And here," said she, "are your fur boots, you will need them in that cold country; the muff I must keep myself, it is too pretty to part with; but you shall not be frozen. Here are my mother's huge gloves; they reach up to the elbow, put them on—now your hands look as clumsy as my old mother's!"

And Gerda shed tears of joy.

"I cannot bear to see you crying!" said the little robber-maiden, "you ought to look glad; see, here are two loaves and a piece of bacon for you, that you may not be hungry on the way." She fastened this provender also on the reindeer's back, opened the door, called away the great dogs, and then cutting asunder with her dagger the rope which bound the reindeer, shouted to him, "Now then, run! but take good care of the little girl."

And Gerda stretched out her hands to the robber-maiden and bade her farewell, and the reindeer fleeted through the forest, over stock and stone, over desert and heath, over meadow and moor. The wolves howled and the ravens shrieked. "Isch! Isch!" A red light flashed—one might have fancied the sky was sneezing.

"Those are my dear old Northern Lights!" said the reindeer; "look at them, how beautiful they are!" And he ran faster than ever—the loaves were eaten, so was the bacon—at last they were in Lapland.

Part Six
The Lapland woman and the Finland woman

THEY stopped at a little hut, a wretched hut it was; the roof very nearly touched the ground, and the door was so low that whoever wished to go either in or out was obliged to crawl upon hands and knees. No one was at home except an old Lapland woman who was busy boiling fish over a lamp filled with train oil. The reindeer related to her Gerda's whole history, not, however, till after he had made her acquainted with his own, which appeared to him of much more importance. Poor Gerda, meanwhile, was so overpowered by the cold that she could not speak.

"Ah, poor things!" said the Lapland woman, "you have still a long way before you! You have a hundred miles to run before you can arrive in Finland: the Snow Queen dwells there, and burns blue lights every evening. I will write for you a few words on a piece of dried stock-fish—paper I have none—and you may take it with you to the wise Finland woman who lives there; she will advise you better than I can."

So when Gerda had well warmed herself and taken some food, the Lapland woman wrote a few words on a dried stock-fish, bade Gerda take care of it, and bound her once more firmly on the reindeer's back.

Onwards they sped; the wondrous Northern Lights, now of the loveliest, brightest blue colour, shone all through the night, and amidst these splendid illuminations they arrived in Finland, and knocked at the chimney of the wise woman, for she had no door to her house.

Hot, very hot was it within—so much so that the wise woman wore scarcely any clothing; she was low in stature and very dirty. She immediately loosened little Gerda's dress, took off her fur boots and thick gloves, laid a piece of ice on the reindeer's head, and then read what was written on the stock-fish. She read it three times. After the third reading she knew it by heart, and threw the fish into the porridge-pot, for it might make a very excellent supper, and she never wasted anything.

The reindeer then repeated his own story, and when that was finished he told of little Gerda's adventures, and the wise woman twinkled her wise eyes, but spoke not a word.

"Thou art so powerful," continued the reindeer, "that I know thou canst twist all the winds of the world into a thread, of which if the pilot loosen one knot he will have a favourable wind; if he loosen the second it will blow sharp, and if he loosen the third, so tremendous a storm will arise that the trees of the forest will be uprooted, and the ship wrecked. Wilt thou not mix for this little maiden that wonderful draught which will give her the strength of twelve men, and thus enable her to overcome the Snow Queen?"

"The strength of twelve men!" repeated the wise woman, "that would be of much use to be sure!" and she walked away, drew forth a large parchment roll from a shelf and began to read. What strange characters were seen inscribed on the scroll as the wise woman slowly unrolled it! She read so intently that the perspiration ran down her forehead.

But the reindeer pleaded so earnestly for little Gerda, and Gerda's eyes were raised so entreatingly and tearfully, that at last the wise woman's eyes began to twinkle again out of sympathy, and she drew the reindeer into a corner, and putting a fresh piece of ice upon his head, whispered thus:

"Little Kay is still with the Snow Queen, in whose abode everything is according to his taste, and therefore he believes it to be the best place in the world. But that is because he has a glass splinter in his heart, and a glass splinter in his eye—until he has got rid of them he will never feel like a human being, and the Snow Queen will always maintain her influence over him."

"But canst thou not give something to little Gerda whereby she may overcome all these evil influences?"

"I can give her no power so great as that which she already possesses. Seest thou not how strong she is? Seest thou not that both men and animals must serve her—a poor little girl wandering barefoot through the world? Her power is greater than ours, it proceeds from her heart, from her being a loving and innocent child. If this power which she already possesses cannot give her access to the Snow Queen's palace, and enable her to free Kay's eye and heart from the glass fragment, we can do nothing for her! Two miles hence is the Snow Queen's garden; thither thou canst carry the little maiden. Put her down close by the bush bearing red berries and half covered with snow: lose no time, and hasten back to this place!"

And the wise woman lifted Gerda on the reindeer's back, and away they went.

"Oh, I have left my boots behind! I have left my gloves behind!" cried little Gerda, when it was too late. The cold was piercing, but the reindeer dared not stop; on he ran until he reached the bush with the red berries. Here he set Gerda down, kissed her, the tears rolling down his cheeks the while, and ran fast back again—which was the best thing he could do. And there stood poor Gerda, without shoes, without gloves, alone in that barren region, that terrible icy-cold Finland.

She ran on as fast as she could; a whole regiment of snow-flakes came to meet her. They did not fall from the sky, which was cloudless and bright with the Northern Lights, they ran straight along the ground, and the farther Gerda advanced the larger they grew. Gerda then remembered how large and curious the snow-flakes had appeared to her when one day she had looked at them through a burning-glass; these, however, were very much larger, they were living forms, they were in fact the Snow Queen's guards. Their shapes were the strangest that could be imagined; some looked like great ugly porcupines, others like snakes rolled into knots with their heads peeping forth, and others like little fat bears with bristling hair—all, however, were alike dazzlingly white—all were living snowflakes. Little Gerda

. . . the wise woman lifted Gerda on the reindeer's back

began to repeat "Our Father"; meanwhile, the cold was so intense that she could see her own breath, which, as it escaped her mouth, ascended into the air like vapour; the cold grew intense, the vapour more dense, and at length took the forms of little bright angels which, as they touched the earth, became larger and more distinct. They wore helmets on their heads, and carried shields and spears in their hands; their number increased so rapidly that, by the time Gerda had finished her prayer, a whole legion stood around her. They thrust with their spears against the horrible snow-flakes, which fell into thousands of pieces, and little Gerda walked on unhurt and undaunted. The angels touched her hands and feet, and then she scarcely felt the cold, and boldly approached the Snow Queen's palace.

But before we accompany her there, let us see what Kay is doing. He is certainly not thinking of little Gerda, least of all can he imagine that she is now standing at the palace gate.

Part Seven
*Which treats of the Snow Queen's palace,
and of what came to pass therein*

THE walls of the palace were formed of the driven snow; its doors and windows of the cutting winds. There were above a hundred halls, the largest of them many miles in extent, all illuminated by the Northern Lights, all alike vast, empty, icily cold, and dazzlingly white. No sounds of mirth ever resounded through these dreary spaces; no cheerful scene refreshed the sight—not even so much as a bear's ball, such as one might imagine sometimes takes place, the tempest forming a band of musicians, and the polar bears standing on their hind paws and exhibiting themselves in the oddest positions. Nor was there ever a card-assembly, wherein the cards might be held in the mouth and dealt out by paws; nor even a small select coffee party for the white young lady foxes. Vast, empty, and cold were the Snow Queen's chambers, and the Northern Lights flashed, now high, now low, in regular gradations. In the midst of the empty, interminable snow saloon lay a frozen lake; it was broken into a thousand pieces, but these pieces so exactly resembled each other, that the breaking of them might well be deemed a work of more than human skill. The Snow Queen, when at home, always sat in the centre of this lake; she used to say that she was then sitting on the Mirror of Reason, and that hers was the best, indeed, the only one, in the world.

Little Kay was quite blue, nay, almost black with cold, but he did not observe it, for the Snow Queen had kissed away the shrinking feeling he used to experience, and his heart was like a lump of ice. He was busied among the sharp icy fragments, laying and joining them together in every possible way, just as people do with what are called Chinese puzzles. Kay could form the most curious and complete figures—this was the ice-puzzle of reason—and in his eyes these figures were of the utmost importance. He often formed whole words, but there was one word he could never succeed in forming—it was Eternity. The Snow Queen had said to him, "When thou canst put that figure together, thou shalt become thine own master, and I will give thee the whole world, and a new pair of skates besides."

But he could never do it.

"Now I am going to the warm countries," said the Snow Queen. "I shall flit through the air, and look into the black cauldrons"—she meant the burning mountains, Etna and Vesuvius. "I shall whiten them a little; that will be good for the citrons and vineyards." So away flew the Snow Queen, leaving Kay sitting all alone in the large empty hall of ice. He looked at the fragments, and thought and thought till his head ached. He sat so still and so stiff that one might have fancied that he too was frozen.

Cold and cutting blew the winds when little Gerda passed through the palace gates, but she repeated her evening prayer, and they immediately sank to rest. She entered the large, cold, empty hall: she saw Kay, she recognised him, she flew upon his neck, she held him fast, and cried, "Kay! dear, dear Kay! I have found thee at last!"

But he sat still as before, cold, silent, motionless; his unkindness wounded poor Gerda deeply. Hot and bitter were the tears she shed, they fell upon his breast, they reached his heart, they thawed the ice and dissolved the tiny splinter of glass within it. He looked at her whilst she sang her hymn—

"Our roses bloom and fade away,
Our Infant Lord abides alway;
May we be blessed His face to see,
And ever little children be!"

Then Kay burst into tears. He wept till the glass splinter floated in his eye and fell with his tears; he knew his old companion immediately, and exclaimed with joy, "Gerda, my dear little Gerda, where hast thou been all this time?—and where have I been?"

He looked around him. "How cold it is here! how wide and empty!" and he embraced Gerda, whilst she laughed and wept by turns. Even the pieces of ice took part in their joy; they danced about merrily, and when they were wearied and lay down they formed of their own accord the mystical letters of which the Snow Queen had said that when Kay could put them together he should be his own master, and that she would give him the whole world, with a new pair of skates besides.

And Gerda kissed his cheeks, whereupon they became fresh and glowing as ever; she kissed his eyes, and they sparkled like her own; she kissed his hands and feet, and he was once more healthy and merry. The Snow Queen might now come home as soon as she liked— it mattered not; Kay's charter of freedom stood written on the mirror in bright icy characters.

They took each other by the hand, and wandered forth out of the palace, talking meanwhile about the aged grandmother and the rose-trees on the roof of their houses; and as they walked on, the winds were hushed into a calm, and the sun burst forth in splendour from among the dark storm-clouds. When they arrived at the bush with the red berries, they found the reindeer standing by awaiting their arrival; he had brought with him another and younger reindeer, whose udders were full, and who gladly gave her warm milk to refresh the young travellers.

The old reindeer and the young hind now carried Kay and Gerda on their backs, first to the little hot room of the wise woman of Finland, where they warmed themselves, and received advice how to proceed in their journey home, and afterwards to the abode of the Lapland woman, who made them some new clothes and provided them with a sledge.

The whole party now ran on together till they came to the boundary of the country; but just where the green leaves began to sprout, the Lapland woman and the two reindeers took their leave. "Farewell! farewell!" said they all. And the first little birds they had seen for many a long day began to chirp, and warble their pretty songs; and the trees of the forest burst upon them full of rich and variously tinted foliage. Suddenly the green boughs parted asunder, and a spirited horse galloped up. Gerda knew it well, for it was the one which had been harnessed to her gold coach; and on it sat a young girl wearing a bright scarlet cap, and with pistols on the holster before her. It was indeed no other than the robber-maiden, who, weary of her home in the forest, was going on her travels, first to the north and afterwards to other parts of the world. She at once recognised Gerda, and Gerda had not forgotten her. Most joyful was their greeting.

"A fine gentleman you are, to be sure, you graceless young truant!" said she to Kay. "I should like to know if you deserved that anyone should be running to the end of the world on your account!"

But Gerda stroked her cheeks, and asked after the prince and princess and their whereabouts.

"They are gone travelling into foreign countries," replied the robber-maiden.

"And the raven?" asked Gerda.

"Ah! the raven is dead," returned she. "The tame beloved has become a widow; so she hops about with a piece of worsted wound round her leg; she moans most piteously, and chatters more than ever! But tell me now all that has happened to you, and how you managed to pick up your old playfellow."

And Gerda and Kay told their story.

"Snip-snap-snurre-basselurre!" said the robber-maiden. She pressed the hands of both, promised that if ever she passed through their town she would pay them a visit, and then bade them farewell, and rode away out into the wide world.

Kay and Gerda walked on hand in hand, and wherever they went it was spring, beautiful spring, with its bright flowers and green leaves.

They arrived at a large town; the church bells were ringing merrily, and they immediately recognised the high towers rising into the sky—it was the town wherein they had lived. Joyfully they passed through the streets, joyfully they stopped at the door of Gerda's grandmother. They walked up the stairs and entered the well-known room. The clock said "Tick, tick!" and the hands moved as before. Only one alternation could they find, and that was in themselves, for they saw that they were now full-grown persons. The rose-trees on the roof blossomed in front of the open window, and there beneath them stood the children's stools. Kay and Gerda went and sat down upon them, still holding each other by the hands; the cold, hollow splendour of the Snow Queen's palace they had forgotten, it seemed to them only an unpleasant dream. The grandmother meanwhile sat amid God's bright sunshine, and read from the Bible these words: "Unless ye become as little children, ye shall not enter into the kingdom of heaven."

And Kay and Gerda gazed on each other; they now understood the words of their hymn—

> "Our roses bloom and fade away,
> Our Infant Lord abides alway;
> May we be blessed His face to see,
> And ever little children be!"

There they sat, those two happy ones, grown-up and yet children— children in heart, while all around them glowed bright summer— warm, glorious summer.

TOMMELISE

ONCE upon a time there lived a young wife who longed exceedingly to possess a little child of her own, so she went to an old witch- woman and said to her, "I wish so very much to have a child, a little tiny child, won't you give me one, old mother?"

"Oh, with all my heart!" replied the witch. "Here is a barley- corn for you; it is not exactly of the same sort as those that grow on the farmer's fields, or that are given to the fowls in the poultry yard, but do you sow it in a flower-pot, and then you shall see what you shall see!"

"Thank you, thank you!" cried the woman, and she gave the witch a silver sixpence, and then having returned home sowed the barley- corn as she had been directed, whereupon a large and beautiful flower immediately shot forth from the flower-pot. It looked like a tulip, but the petals were tightly folded up; it was still in bud.

"What a lovely flower!" exclaimed the peasant-woman, and she kissed the pretty red and yellow leaves, and as she kissed them the flower gave a loud report and opened. It was indeed a tulip, but on the small green pointal in the centre of the flower there sat a little tiny girl, so pretty and delicate, but her whole body scarcely bigger than the young peasant's thumb. So she called her Tommelise.

A pretty varnished walnut-shell was given her as a cradle, blue violet leaves served as her mattresses, and a rose-leaf was her coverlet; here she slept at night, but in the daytime she played on the table. The peasant-wife had filled a plate with water, and laid flowers in it, their blossoms bordering the edge of the plate, while the stalks lay in the water; on the surface floated a large tulip-leaf, and on it Tommelise might sit and sail from one side of the plate to the other, two white horse hairs having been given her for oars. That looked quite charming! And Tommelise could sing too, and she sang in such low sweet tones as never were heard before.

One night, while she was lying in her pretty bed, a great ugly toad came hopping in through the broken window-pane. The toad was such a great creature, old and withered-looking, and wet too; she hopped at once down upon the table where Tommelise lay sleeping under the red rose petal.

"That is just the wife for my son," said the toad; and she seized hold of the walnut-shell, with Tommelise in it, and hopped away with her through the broken pane down into the garden. Here flowed a broad stream; its banks were muddy and swampy, and it was amongst this mud that the old toad and her son dwelt. Ugh, how hideous and deformed he was! just like his mother.

"Coax, coax, brekke-ke-kex!" was all he could find to say on seeing the pretty little maiden in the walnut-shell.

"Don't make such a riot, or you'll wake her!" said old mother toad. "She may easily run away from us, for she is as light as a swan-down feather. I'll tell you what we'll do; we'll take her out into the brook, and set her down on one of the large water-lily leaves; it will be like an island to her, who is so light and small. Then she cannot run away from us, and we can go and get ready the state-rooms down under the mud, where you and she are to dwell together."

Out in the brook there grew many water-lilies, with their broad green leaves, each of which seemed to be floating over the water. The leaf which was the farthest from the shore was also the largest; to it swam old mother toad, and on it she set the walnut-shell, with Tommelise.

The poor little tiny creature awoke quite early next morning, and, when she saw where she was, she began to weep most bitterly, for there was nothing but water on all sides, of the large green leaf, and she could in no way reach the land.

Old mother toad was down in the mud, decorating her apartments with bulrushes and yellow buttercups, so as to make them quite gay and tidy to receive her new daughter-in-law. At last, she and her frightful son swam together to the leaf where she had left Tommelise; they wanted to fetch her pretty cradle, and place it for her in the bridal chamber before she herself was conducted into it. Old mother toad bowed low in the water, and said to her, "Here is my son, he is to be thy husband, and you will dwell together so comfortably down in the mud!"

"Coax, coax, brekk-ke-kex!" was all that her son could say.

Then they took the neat little bed and swam away with it, whilst Tommelise sat alone on the green leaf, weeping, for she did not like the thought of living with the withered old toad, and having her ugly son for a husband. The little fishes that were swimming to and fro in the water beneath had heard what mother toad had said, so they now put up their heads—they wanted to see the little maid. And when they saw her, they were charmed with her delicate beauty, and it vexed them very much that the hideous old toad should carry her off. No, that should never be! They surrounded the green stalk in the water, whereon rested the water-lily leaf and gnawed it asunder with their teeth, and then the leaf floated away down the brook, with Tommelise on it; away, far away, where the old toad could not follow.

Tommelise sailed past so many places, and the wild birds among the bushes saw her and sang, "Oh, what a sweet little maiden!" On and on, farther and farther, floated the leaf: Tommelise was on her travels.

A pretty little white butterfly kept fluttering round and round her, and at last settled down on the leaf, for he loved Tommelise very much, and she was so pleased. There was nothing to trouble her now that she had no fear of the old toad pursuing her, and wherever she sailed everything was so beautiful, for the sun shone down on the water, making it bright as liquid gold. And now she took off her sash, and tied one end of it round the butterfly, fastening the other end firmly into the leaf. On floated the leaf, faster and faster, and Tommelise with it.

Presently a great cock-chafer came buzzing past; he caught sight of her, and immediately fastening his claw round her slender waist, flew up into a tree with her. But the green leaf still floated down the brook, and the butterfly with it; he was bound to the leaf and could not get loose.

Oh, how terrified was poor Tommelise when the cock-chafer carried her up into the tree, and how sorry she felt, too, for the darling white butterfly which she had left tied fast to the leaf; she feared that if he could not get away, he would perish of hunger. But the cock-chafer cared nothing for that. He settled with her upon the largest leaf in the tree, gave her some honey from the flowers to eat, and hummed her praises, telling her she was very pretty, although she was not at all like a hen-chafer. And by-and-by all the chafers who lived in that tree came to pay her a visit; they looked at Tommelise, and one Miss Hen-chafer drew in her feelers, saying, "She has only two legs, how miserable that looks!" "She has no feelers," cried another. "And see how thin and lean her waist is; why, she is just like a human being!" observed a third. "How very, very ugly she is!" at last cried all the lady-chafers in chorus. The chafer who had carried off Tommelise still could not persuade himself that she was otherwise than pretty, but, as all the rest kept repeating and insisting that she was ugly, he at last began to think they must be in the right, and determined to have nothing more to do with her; she might go whenever she would, for aught he cared, he said. And so the whole swarm flew down from the tree with her, and set her on a daisy; then she wept because she was so ugly that the lady-chafers would not keep company with her, and yet Tommelise was the prettiest little creature that could be imagined, soft and delicate and transparent as the loveliest rose-leaf.

All the summer long poor Tommelise lived alone in the wide wood. She wove herself a bed of grass-straw, and hung it under a large burdock-leaf which sheltered her from the rain; she dined off the honey from the flowers, and drank from the dew that every morning spangled the leaves and herblets around her. Thus passed the summer and autumn, but then came winter, the cold, long winter. All the birds who had sung so sweetly to her flew away, trees and flowers withered, the large burdock-leaf under which Tommelise had lived, rolled itself up, and became a dry, yellow stalk, and Tommelise was fearfully cold, for her clothes were wearing out, and she herself was so slight and frail, poor little thing! she was nearly frozen to death. It began to snow, and every light flake that fell upon her made her feel as we should if a whole shovelful of snow were thrown upon us, for we are giants in comparison with a little creature only an inch long. She wrapped herself up in a withered leaf, but it gave her no warmth; she shuddered with cold.

Close outside the wood, on the skirt of which Tommelise had been living, lay a large corn-field, but the corn had been carried away long ago, leaving only the dry, naked stubble standing up from the hard-frozen earth. It was like another wood to Tommelise, and oh, how she shivered with cold as she made her way through. At last she came past the field-mouse's door; for the field-mouse had made herself a little hole under the stubble, and there she dwelt snugly and comfortably, having a room full of corn, and a neat kitchen and store-chamber besides. And poor Tommelise must now play the beggar-girl; she stood at the door and begged for a little piece of a barley-corn, for she had had nothing to eat during two whole days.

"Thou poor little thing!" said the field-mouse, who was indeed a thoroughly good-natured old creature, "come into my warm room and dine with me."

And as she soon took a great liking to Tommelise, she proposed to her to stay. "You may dwell with me all the winter if you will, but keep my room clean and neat, and tell me stories, for I love stories dearly."

And Tommelise did all that the kind old field-mouse required of her, and was made very comfortable in her new abode.

"We shall have a visitor presently," observed the field-mouse; "my next-door neighbour comes to see me once every week. He is better off than I am, has large rooms in his house, and wears a coat of such beautiful black velvet. It would be a capital thing for you if you could secure him for your husband, but unfortunately he is blind, he cannot see you. You must tell him the prettiest stories you know."

But Tommelise did not care at all about pleasing their neighbour Mr. Mole, nor did she wish to marry him. He came and paid a visit in his black velvet suit, he was so rich and so learned, and the field-mouse declared his domestic offices were twenty times larger than hers; but the sun and the pretty flowers he could not endure, he was always abusing them, though he had never seen either. Tommelise was called upon to sing for his amusement, and by the time she had sung "Lady-bird, lady-bird, fly away home!" and "The Friar of Orders Grey", the mole had quite fallen in love with her through the charm of her sweet voice; however, he said nothing, he was such a prudent, cautious animal.

He had just been digging a long passage through the earth from their house to his, and he now gave permission to the field-mouse and Tommelise to walk in it as often as they liked; however, he bade them not be afraid of the dead bird that lay in the passage; it was a whole bird, with beak and feathers entire, and therefore he supposed it must have died quite lately, at the beginning of the winter, and had been buried just in the place where he had dug his passage.

The mole took a piece of tinder, which shines like fire in the dark, in his mouth, and went on first to light his friends through the long dark passage, and when they came to the place where the dead bird lay, he thrust his broad nose up against the ceiling and pushed up the earth, so as to make a great hole for the light to come through. In the midst of the floor lay a swallow, his wings clinging firmly to his sides, his head and legs drawn under the feathers; the poor bird had evidently died of cold. Tommelise felt so very sorry, for she loved all the little birds, who had sung and chirped so merrily to her the whole summer long; but the mole kicked it with his short legs, saying, "Here's a fine end to all its whistling! a miserable thing it must to be to be born a bird. None of my children will be birds, that's a comfort! Such creatures have nothing but their 'quivit,' and must be starved to death in the winter."

"Yes, indeed, a sensible animal like you may well say so," returned the field-mouse; "what has the bird got by all his chirping and chirruping? when winter comes it must starve and freeze; and it is such a great creature too!"

Tommelise said nothing, but when the two others had turned their backs upon the bird, she bent over it, smoothed down the feathers that covered its head, and kissed the closed eyes. "Perhaps it was this one that sang so delightfully to me in the summer time," thought she; "how much pleasure it has given me, the dear, dear bird!"

The mole now stopped up the hole through which the daylight had pierced, and then followed the ladies home. But Tommelise could not sleep that night, so she got out of her bed, and wove a carpet out of hay, and then went out and spread it round the dead bird; she also fetched some soft cotton from the field-mouse's room, which she laid over the bird, that it might be warm amid the cold earth.

"Farewell, thou dear bird," said she; "farewell, and thanks for thy beautiful song in the summer time, when all the trees were green, and the sun shone so warmly upon us!" And she pressed her head against the bird's breast, but was terrified to feel something beating within it. It was the bird's heart, the bird was not dead; it had lain in a swoon, and now that it was warmer its life returned.

Every autumn all the swallows fly away to warm countries; but if one of them lingers behind, it freezes and falls down as though dead, and the cold snow covers it.

Tommelise trembled with fright, for the bird was very large compared with her, who was only an inch in length. However, she took courage, laid the cotton more closely round the poor swallow, and fetching a leaf which had served herself as a coverlet, spread it over the bird's head.

The next night she stole out again, and found that the bird's life had quite returned, though it was so feeble that only for one short moment could it open its eyes to look at Tommelise, who stood by with a piece of tinder in her hand—she had no other lantern.

"Thanks to thee, thou sweet little child!" said the sick swallow. "I feel delightfully warm now; soon I shall recover my strength, and be able to fly again, out in the warm sunshine."

"Oh no," she replied, "it is too cold without, it snows and freezes! thou must stay in thy warm bed, I will take care of thee."

She brought the swallow water in a flower-petal and he drank, and then he told her how he had torn one of his wings in a thorn bush, and therefore could not fly fast enough to keep up with the other swallows who were all migrating to the warm countries. He had at last fallen to the earth, and more than that he could not remember; he did not at all know how he had got under ground.

However, under ground he remained all the winter long, and Tommelise was kind to him, and loved him dearly, but she never said a word about him either to the mole or the field-mouse, for she knew they could not endure the poor swallow.

As soon as the spring came and the sun's warmth had penetrated the earth, the swallow said farewell to Tommelise, and she opened

She brought the swallow water in a flower-petal

for him the covering of earth which the mole had thrown back before. The sun shone in upon them so deliciously, and the swallow asked whether she would not go with him; she might sit upon his back, and then they would fly together far out into the greenwood. But Tommelise knew it would vex the old field-mouse if she were to leave her.

"No, I cannot, I must not go," said Tommelise.

"Fare thee well, then, thou good and pretty maiden," said the swallow, and away he flew into the sunshine. Tommelise looked after him and the tears came into her eyes, for she loved the poor swallow so much.

"Quivit, quivit," sang the bird, as he flew into the greenwood. And Tommelise was now sad indeed. She was not allowed to go out into the warm sunshine; the wheat that had been sown in the field above the field-mouse's house grew up so high that it seemed a perfect forest to the poor little damsel who was only an inch in stature.

"This summer you must work at getting your wedding clothes ready," said the field-mouse, for their neighbour, the blind dull mole in the black velvet suit, had now made his proposals in form to Tommelise. "You shall have worsted and linen in plenty; you shall be well provided with all manner of clothes and furniture before you become the mole's wife." So Tommelise was obliged to work hard at the distaff, and the field-mouse hired four spiders to spin and weave night and day. Every evening came the mole, and always began to talk about the summer soon coming to an end, and that then, when the sun would no longer shine so warmly, scorching the earth till it was as dry as a stone, yes, then, his nuptials with Tommelise should take place. But this sort of conversation did not please her at all, she was thoroughly wearied of his dullness and his prating. Every morning when the sun rose, and every evening when it set, she used to steal out at the door, and when the wind blew the tops of the corn aside, so that she could see the blue sky through the opening, she thought how bright and beautiful it was out here, and wished most fervently to see the dear swallow once more; but he never came, he must have been flying far away in the beautiful greenwood.

Autumn came, and Tommelise's wedding clothes were ready.

"Four weeks more, and you shall be married!" said the field-mouse. But Tommelise wept, and said she would not marry the dull mole.

"Fiddlestick!" exclaimed the field-mouse; "don't be obstinate, child, or I shall bite thee with my white teeth! Is he not handsome, pray? Why, the queen has not got such a black velvet dress as he wears! And isn't he rich? rich both in kitchens and cellars? Be thankful to get such a husband!"

So Tommelise must be married. The day fixed had arrived, the mole had already come to fetch his bride, and she must dwell with him, deep under the earth, never again to come out into the warm sunshine which she loved so much, and which he could not endure. The poor child was in despair at the thought that she must now bid farewell to the beautiful sun of which she had at least been allowed to catch a glimpse every now and then while she lived with the field-mouse.

"Farewell, thou glorious sun!" she cried, throwing her arms up into the air, and she walked on a little way beyond the field-mouse's door; the corn was already reaped, and only the dry stubble surrounded her. "Farewell, farewell!" repeated she, as she clasped her tiny arms round a little red flower that grew there. "Greet the dear swallow from me, if thou shouldst see him."

"Quivit! quivit!"—there was a fluttering of wings just over her head; she looked up, and behold! the little swallow was flying past. And how pleased he was when he perceived Tommelise! She told how that she had been obliged to accept the disagreeable mole as a husband, and that she would have to dwell deep under ground where the sun never pierced. And she could not help weeping as she spoke.

"The cold winter will soon be here!" said the swallow; "I shall fly far away to the warm countries. Wilt thou go with me? Thou canst sit on my back, and tie thyself firmly to me with thy sash, and thus we shall fly away from the stupid mole and his dark room, far away over the mountains to those countries where the sun shines so brightly, where it is always summer, and flowers blossom all the year round. Come and fly with me, thou sweet little Tommelise, who didst save my life when I lay frozen in the dark cellars of the earth!"

"Yes, I will go with thee!" said Tommelise. And she seated herself on the bird's back, her feet resting on the outspread wings, and tied her girdle firmly round one of the strongest feathers, and then the swallow soared high into the air, and flew away over forest and over lake, over mountains whose crests are covered with snow all the year round. How Tommelise shivered as she breathed the keen frosty air! However, she soon crept down under the bird's warm feathers, her head still peering forth, eager to behold all the glory and beauty beneath her. At last they reached the warm countries. There the sun shone far more brightly than in her native clime. The heavens seemed twice as high, and twice as blue; and ranged along the sloping hills grew, in rich luxuriance, the loveliest green and purple grapes. Citrons and melons were seen in the groves, the fragrance of myrtles and balsams filled the air, and by the wayside gambolled groups of pretty merry children, chasing large bright-winged butterflies.

But the swallow did not rest here; still he flew on; and still the scene seemed to grow more and more beautiful. Near a calm, blue lake, overhung by lofty trees, stood a half-ruined palace of white marble, built in times long past; vine-wreaths trailed up the long slender pillars, and on the capitals, among the green leaves and waving tendrils, many a swallow had built his nest, and one of these nests belonged to the swallow on whose back Tommelise was riding.

"This is my house," said the swallow, "but if thou wouldst rather choose for thyself one of the splendid flowers growing beneath us, and thou shalt make thy home in the loveliest of them all."

"That will be charming!" exclaimed she, clapping her tiny hands.

On the green turf beneath there lay the fragments of a white marble column which had fallen to the ground, and around these fragments twined some beautiful large white flowers. The swallow flew down with Tommelise, and set her on one of the broad petals. But what was her surprise when she saw sitting in the very heart of the flower a little mannikin, fair and transparent as though he were made of glass! wearing the prettiest gold crown on his head, and the brightest, most delicate wings on his shoulders, yet scarcely one whit larger than Tommelise herself. He was the spirit of the flower. In every blossom there dwelt one such faery youth or maiden, but this one was the king of all these flower-spirits.

"Oh, how handsome he is, this king!" whispered Tommelise to the swallow. The faery prince was quite startled at the sudden descent of the swallow, who was a sort of giant compared with him; but when he saw Tommelise he was delighted, for she was the very loveliest maiden he had ever seen. So he took his gold crown off his own head and set it upon hers, asked her name, and whether she would be his bride, and reign as queen over all the flower-spirits. This, you see, was quite a different bridegroom from the son of the ugly old toad, or the blind mole with his black velvet coat. So Tommelise replied "Yes" to the beautiful prince, and then the lady and gentlemen faeries came out, each from a separate flower, to pay their homage to Tommelise; so gracefully and courteously they paid their homage! and every one of them brought her a present.

But the best of all the presents was a pair of transparent wings; they were fastened on Tommelise's shoulders, and enabled her to fly from flower to flower.

That was the greatest of pleasures; and the little swallow sat in his nest above and sang to her his sweetest song; in his heart, however, he was very sad, for he loved Tommelise, and would have wished never to part from her.

"Thou shalt no longer be called Tommelise," said the king of flowers to her, "for it is not a pretty name, and thou art so lovely! We will call thee Maia."

"Farewell! farewell!" sang the swallow, and away he flew from the warm countries, far away back to Denmark. There he had a little nest just over the window of the man who writes stories for children. "Quivit, quivit, quivit!" he sang to him, and from him we have learned this history.

GREAT CLAUS AND LITTLE CLAUS

ONCE upon a time there lived in the same village two men bearing the very same name. One of them chanced to possess four horses, the other had only one horse, so, by way of distinguishing them from each other, the proprietor of four horses was called "Great Claus", and he who owned but one horse was known as "Little Claus". And now we shall relate their true and veritable history.

All the week long Little Claus had to plough for Great Claus, and to lend him his one horse, and in return Great Claus lent him his four horses, but only for one day in the week, and that day was Sunday. Hurrah! a proud man then was Little Claus, and how he brandished his whip over his five horses, for all five were his, he thought, for this one day at least. And the sun shone so brightly, and all the bells in the church tower were ringing; the people were dressed in their best and walking to church, and as they passed they looked at Little Claus, who was driving his five horses, and he was so pleased that he kept cracking his whip again and again, crying out the while, "Hip, hip, hurrah! five fine horses, and all of them mine!"

"You must not say that," observed Great Claus; "only one of the horses is yours, you know that well enough."

But when another party of church-goers passed close by him, Little

Claus quite forgot that he had been told he must not say so, and cried out again, "Hip, hip, hurrah! five fine horses, all mine!"

"Did not I tell you to hold your tongue?" exclaimed Great Claus, very angrily. "If you say that again, I'll give your one horse such a blow on the forehead as shall strike him dead on the spot, and then there'll soon be an end to your boasting about your five fine horses."

"Oh, but I'll never say it again, indeed I won't!" said Little Claus, and he quite intended to keep his word. But presently some more people came by, and when they nodded a friendly "good morning" to him, he was so delighted, and it seemed to him such a grand thing to have five horses to plough his bit of a field, that he really could not contain himself, he flourished his whip aloft, and shouted out, "Hip, hip, hurrah! five fine horses, every one of them mine!"

"I'll soon cure you of that!" cried Great Claus, in a fury, and, taking up a large stone, he flung it at the head of Little Claus' horse —so heavy was the stone that the poor creature fell down dead.

"Alas, now I have no horses at all!" cried Little Claus, and he began to weep. As soon as he had recovered himself a little, he set to work to flay the skin off his dead horse, dried the skin thoroughly in the air, and then putting it into a sack, he slung the sack across his shoulders, and set out on his way to the nearest town, intending to sell the skin. He had a long way to go, and the road led him through a large and thickly-grown wood. And here a violent tempest burst forth; the clouds, the rain, and the dark firs, bowed to and fro by the wind, so bewildered poor Claus that he lost his path, and before he could recover it, evening had darkened into night; he could neither return homewards nor get on to the town. However, not far off stood a large farm-house; the window-shutters were closed, but Little Claus could see lights shining out through the cracks. "Perhaps I may get shelter there," thought he, so he went up to the house, and knocked at the door. The farmer's wife came and opened it to him, but when she heard what he wanted, she very obligingly told him he must go and ask elsewhere; he shouldn't come into her house; her good man was from home, and she couldn't be receiving strangers in his absence.

"Well, then, I must sleep outside, under this stormy sky," replied Little Claus, and the farmer's wife shut the door in his face.

Close by stood a hay-stack, and between it and the house there was a little pent-house with a flat straw roof.

"I'll get up there," said Little Claus to himself, on perceiving this; "it will make me a capital bed—only I do hope the stork yonder may not take it into his head to fly down and bite my legs," for a stork had made his nest on the roof, and had mounted guard beside the nest, as wide-awake as could be, although it was night.

So Little Claus crept up on the pent-house, and there he turned and twisted about till he had made himself a right comfortable couch. The window-shutters did not close properly at the top, so that from his high and airy position he could see all that went on in the room.

There he saw a large table spread with bread and wine, roast meat and fried fish. The farmer's wife and the sexton sat at table; no one else was there; the farmer's wife was pouring out a glass of wine for the sexton, who, meantime, was eagerly helping himself to a large slice of the fish—he happened to be particularly fond of fish.

"Too bad, really, to keep it all to themselves!" sighed Little Claus. "If they would but give me a little, wee morsel!" and he stretched out his head as near to the window as he could. Oh, what a magnificent cake he could see now! Why, this was quite a banquet!

Presently he heard the sound of hoof-tramps approaching from the road. It was the farmer riding home.

A regularly good-hearted fellow was this farmer, but he had one peculiar weakness, namely that he never could endure to see a sexton; the sight made him half mad. Now, the sexton of the neighbouring town happened to be first cousin to his wife, and they were old play-mates and good friends, so, this evening, knowing that the farmer would be from home, he came to play his cousin a visit, and the good woman, being very pleased to see him, had brought out all the choice things in her larder, wherewith to regale him. But now, while they were sitting together so comfortably, they heard the tramp of the farmer's horse; they both started up, and the woman bade the sexton creep into a large empty chest that stood in a corner of the room. He did so, for he knew that the poor farmer would be almost driven wild if he came in and saw a sexton standing unexpectedly before him. And the farmer's wife then made a bustle to hide all the wine and the dishes inside her baking-oven, for fear her husband, if he saw the table spread with them, should ask for whom she had been preparing such a grand entertainment.

"Oh dear, oh dear!" sighed Little Claus from his couch on the pent-house, when he saw the feast all put on one side.

"Anybody up there?" inquired the farmer, on hearing the voice; and he looked up and perceived Little Claus. "Why are you lying there? Come down into the house with me."

And Little Claus explained that he had lost his way, and asked the farmer if he would not give him shelter for the night.

"To be sure I will," replied the good-natured man. "Come in quickly, and let's have something to eat."

The woman received them both with a great show of welcome, covered one end of the long table, and brought out a large dish of oatmeal. The farmer set to with a capital appetite, but Little Claus could not eat for thinking of the good roast meat, the fish, the wine, and the delicious cake which he had seen stowed away inside the oven.

He put his sack containing the horse's skin under the table, and now, as he could not relish the oatmeal porridge, he began trampling the sack under his feet till the dry skin creaked aloud.

"Hush!" muttered Little Claus, as if speaking to his sack, but at the same moment be trod upon it again, so as to make it creak louder than before.

"What have you got in your sack?" asked the farmer.

"Oh! I've got a little conjuror there," replied Little Claus, "and he says we are not to be eating oatmeal porridge any longer, for he has conjured a feast of beef-steak, fried fish, and cake, into the oven on purpose for us."

"A conjuror, did you say?" exclaimed the farmer, and up he got in a vast hurry to look into the oven and see whether the conjuror had spoken truly. And there, to be sure, were fish, and steak, and cake; the conjuror had been as good as his word. The farmer's wife durst not utter a syllable of explanation; almost as much bewildered as her husband, she set the viands on the table, and the farmer and his guest began with a hearty appetite to eat of the good cheer before them.

Presently Little Claus trampled on his sack again, and again made the skin creak.

"What does your conjuror say now?" asked the farmer.

"He says," replied Little Claus, "that he has also conjured three bottles of wine here for us; you will find them standing just in the corner of the oven." So the woman was now obliged to bring out the wine that she had concealed, and the farmer poured himself out a glass and began to think it would be a fine thing to have such a capital conjuror as this.

"A right proper sort of conjuror this of yours!" observed he at last. "I should rather like to see him; will he let me, do you think?"

"Oh, of course," returned Little Claus; "my conjuror will do anything I ask him. That you will, won't you?" asked he, again treading on his sack. "Didn't your hear him say 'Yes'? But I warn you he will look somewhat dark and unpleasing; after all, it is scarcely worth while to see him!"

"Oh, I shall not be afraid. What will he look like?"

"Why, he will appear for all the world just like a sexton."

"A sexton!" repeated the farmer, "that is a pity! You must know that I cannot endure the sight of a sexton; but no matter, since I shall know that it is not a real sexton, but only your conjuror, I shall not care about it. Oh, I've plenty of courage, only don't let him come too near me!"

"Well, I'll speak to my conjuror about it again," said Little Claus, and he trod on his skin till it went "creak, creak, creak," and bent his ear down as though to listen.

"What does he say now?"

"He says he will transport himself into yonder chest in the corner; you have only to lift up the lid, and there you will see him, but you must mind and shut the lid close down again."

"Will you help me to hold up the lid? it is very heavy," said the farmer, and he went up to the chest wherein his wife had concealed the real sexton, who sat with his limbs huddled up, trembling, and holding his breath, lest he should be discovered; certainly in no very comfortable state.

The farmer gently raised the lid of the chest and peeped under it. "Ugh!" cried he, and immediately started back in affright. "Oh dear, oh dear! I saw him; he looked exactly like our sexton in the town— oh, how horrible!"

However, he sat down at table again, and began to drink glass after glass of wine, by way of recovering from the shock. The wine soon revived his fallen courage. Neither he nor his guest ever thought of going to bed; there they sat, talking and feasting, till late in the night.

"Did you ever see your conjuror before?" inquired the farmer of Little Claus.

"Not I," replied Little Claus, "I should never have thought of asking him to show himself, if you had not proposed it. He knows he is not handsome—he does not wish to obtrude himself into any company; he talks to me, and I to him, and isn't that enough?"

"Oh, indeed, it is!" rejoined the farmer quickly. Then after a minute's hesitation he went on, "Do you know, I should like very much to have your conjuror; would you mind selling him to me? Name your own price; I don't care if I give you a whole bushelful

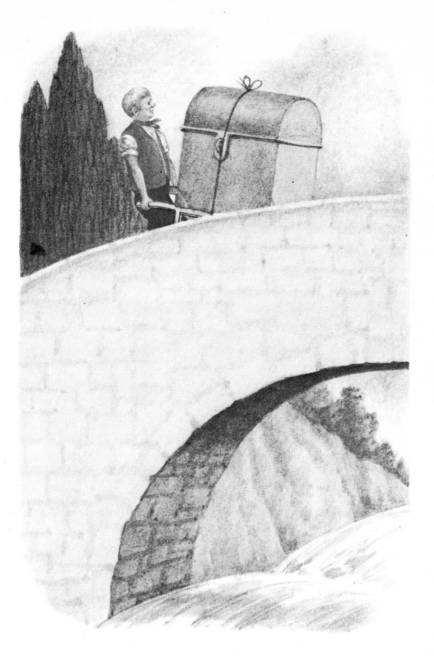

Little Claus took his way over the bridge

of silver on the spot if only you'll give him to me.

"Oh, how can you ask such a thing?" exclaimed Little Claus; "such a useful, such a faithful servant as he is to me, how could I think of parting with him? Why, he's worth his weight in gold ten times over."

"I can't offer you gold," replied the farmer, "but I should like so very much to have him! that is, provided he would never show his ugly self to me again."

"Oh, no fear of that," said Little Claus; "and really, since you have been so kind as to give me shelter to-night, I do not think I can refuse you any request. I will let you have my conjuror for a bushel of silver—only the bushel must be crammed full, you know."

"Certainly it shall," answered the farmer, "and the chest yonder too, you shall have that into the bargain; I don't want it to remain an hour longer in the house, it will always be reminding me of the odious sexton-face I saw inside it."

So the bargain was struck, and Little Claus gave the farmer his sack, with the dry skin in it, and received instead a whole bushelful of silver. The farmer also gave him a large wheel-barrow wherewith to convey home his money and his chest.

"Farewell!" said Little Claus, and away he drove the wheelbarrow, the unfortunate sexton still lying concealed in the chest.

On the opposite side of the wood flowed a broad, deep river: the current was so strong that no one could swim against it, so a bridge had lately been built over it. Little Claus took his way over the bridge, but stopped short in the middle of it, saying very loud, on purpose that the man in the chest might hear him, "Now, what on earth can be the use of this great tumble-down chest to me? and it's as heavy, too, as if it were filled with stones; it quite tires me out. I'll fling it out into the river; if it chooses to float it homewards to me, well and good, if not, it may let it alone; all the same to me."

And he lifted the chest as though intending to throw it into the water.

"Oh, pray don't do that," cried the sexton in the chest; "let me out first, pray."

"Holloa!" exclaimed Little Claus; "is the chest bewitched? If so, the sooner it's off my hands the better."

"Oh, no, no, no," cried the sexton; "let me out, and I'll give you another whole bushelful of money."

"Ah, that's quite another matter," said Little Claus; and he immediately set down the chest, and lifted the lid. Out crept the sexton, greatly to his own satisfaction. He kicked the empty chest into the water, and then took Little Claus to his house with him, where he gave him the bushelful of money, as agreed. Little Claus had now a wheelbarrow full of money.

"Certainly, I must own I have been well paid for my horse's skin," said he to himself, as he entered his own little room, and overturned all his money in a great heap on the floor. "It will vex Great Claus, I'm afraid, when he finds out how rich my horse's skin has made me."

And now he sent a little boy to Great Claus to borrow a measure of him.

"What can he want with a measure, I wonder?" thought Great Claus, and he cunningly smeared the bottom of the measure with clay, hoping that some part of whatever was measured might cleave to the clay. And accordingly, when the measure was returned to him, he discovered three silver coins sticking to the bottom. "Fine doings, upon my word," exclaimed Great Claus, in amazement; and off he set forthwith to the house of his namesake. "Where did you get all that money?" thundered he.

"Oh, I got it by my horse's skin, which I sold yesterday," was the reply.

"Really?" exclaimed Great Claus; "what, are horses' skins so dear as that? Who would have thought it?" And he ran quickly home, took an axe, and struck all his four horses on the head with it, then flayed off the skins, and drove into the town. "Skins, skins, who will buy skins?" cried he, as he passed through the streets.

All the shoemakers and tanners in the town came running up to him, and asked his price.

"I will have a bushelful of money for each," replied Great Claus.

"Are you mad?" cried they. "Do you think we reckon our money by bushels?"

"Skins, fresh skins, who will buy skins?" shouted he again; and still to all who asked how much he wanted for them, he replied, "A bushelful of money."

"The rude boor! he is trying to make fools of us," declared one of his customers at last in very great wrath.

"Skins, fresh skins, fine fresh skins," cried they all, mimicking him. "Out of the town with him, the great ass! or he shall have no skin left on his own shoulders." And Great Claus was ignominiously thrust out of the town, and returned home in no very good humour.

"Little Claus shall pay for this," muttered he. "Sleep soundly this night, Little Claus, for thou shalt hardly wake again."

It so chanced that Little Claus' grandmother died that same evening; she had always been very cross and ill-natured to him in her lifetime, but now, on finding her dead, he felt really sorry for her. He laid the dead woman in his own warm bed in hopes that the warmth might bring her to life again; for his own part, he thought he could spend the night in a chair in a corner of the room; he had often done so before. About midnight the door opened, and Great Claus, his axe in his hand, came in. He knew well where Little Claus' bed was wont to stand; he went straight up to it, and struck the dead grandmother a violent blow on the forehead.

"There's for you," cried he, "now you'll never make a fool of me again," and herewith he went out of the room and returned home.

"What a very wicked man he is," sighed Little Claus. "So he wanted to kill me; it was a good thing that old grandmother was dead already, or that blow would have hurt her very much."

The next day, in the evening, he met Great Claus in a lane near the village. Great Claus started back and stared at him. "What, aren't you dead? I thought I killed you last night."

"Yes, you wicked man," replied Little Claus; "I know you came into my room intending to kill me, but my grandmother, not I, was lying in bed; it was she that you struck with your pickaxe, and you deserve to be hanged for it."

"And are you going to tell people about it?" said Great Claus; "that you never shall!" He was carrying a very large sack; he seized Little Claus by the waist and thrust him into the sack, crying out, "I will drown thee at once, and that will be the end of thy tale-telling."

But he had a long way to walk before he reached the river, and Little Claus was by no means a light burden. The road led past the church, the organ was playing, for the service had just begun. Among the congregation Great Claus saw a man he wanted to speak to; "Little Claus cannot get out of the sack by himself," thought he, "and no one can help him, for all the people are in church. I can just go in and call that man back into the porch for a minute." So she set down the heavy sack and ran into church.

"Oh dear, oh dear!" sighed Little Claus inside the sack; he turned and twisted in vain, it was not possible for him to get the string loose. Just then a very, very old cattle-driver passed by, his hair white as snow, and with a stout staff in his hand; he was driving a large herd of cows and bullocks before him, many more than he, feeble as he was, could manage. One of them rushed up against the sack, and turned it over and over. "Oh, help me, pray!" cried Little Claus, "I am so young to die; help me out of the sack."

"What, is there a man in the sack?" And the ancient cattle-driver bent down, though with some difficulty, and untied the string. "The bullock has not hurt you, I hope?" But Little Claus sprang out so briskly as showed he was not hurt, and set himself immediately to rooting up the withered stump of a tree which stood by the roadside, and which he rolled into the sack, then tying the string he placed the sack exactly as Great Claus had left it. The cattle had, meantime, passed on.

"Will you not drive these cattle home to the village for me?" asked the old man. "I am so weary, and I want to go into church so much."

"Right gladly will I help you since you have helped me," replied Little Claus, and he took the cattle-driver's goad from his hand, and followed the herd in his stead.

Presently Great Claus came running back again. He took up the sack, and again flung it across his shoulders, thinking, "How much lighter the burden seems now; it always does one good to rest for ever so short a time." So on he trudged to the river, flung the sack out into the water, and shouted after it, "There now, Little Claus, you shall never cheat me any more!" He then turned homewards, but on passing a spot where several roads crossed, who should he meet but Little Claus himself with his herd of cattle.

"How comes this?" exclaimed Great Claus; "is it really you? Did I not drown you then, after all?"

"I believe you meant to drown me," said Little Claus; "you threw me into the river just half-an-hour ago, did you not?"

"But how did you come by all these beautiful cattle?" asked Great Claus, in utter amazement, his eyes wandering admiringly from one to another of the herd.

"These are sea-cattle," said Little Claus. "Ah, I'll tell you the whole story! I am really much obliged to you for drowning me; it has made me richer than ever, as you may see. I was so frightened when I lay in the sack, and the wind whistled so uncomfortably into my ears when you threw me down from the bridge into the cold water! I sank to the bottom at once, but I was not hurt, for I was received by the softest, freshest grass. Immediately the sack was opened, and the most beautiful young girl you can imagine, clad in snow-white robes, and with a green wreath in her wet hair, took me by the hand, saying, 'Art thou Little Claus? Here are some cattle of thine, and a mile farther up the road, another and larger herd is grazing, and I will give thee that herd also!' And then I understood that the river was a sort of high-road for the people of the sea, and that on it they walked and drove to and fro from the sea far up into the land where the river rises, and thence back to the sea again. And no place can be more beautiful than it is at the bottom of the water. The prettiest flowers and the freshest grass grow there, and the fishes swimming in the water slipped to and fro about my ears just as birds flutter about us up here in the air. And such gaily-dressed people I saw there, and such a multitude of catle grazing in pastures enclosed with hedges and ditches!"

"Then why were you in such a hurry to come up again?" inquired Great Claus. "I shouldn't have done so, not I, when I found it so pleasant there."

"Ah," rejoined Little Claus; "that was so cleverly done on my part! Did not I tell you that the sea-lady told me that a mile up the road—and by the road she could only mean the river, she can't come into our land roads—there was another and larger herd of cattle for me? But I knew that the river makes a great many turns and windings, and therefore I thought I'd just spare myself half a mile of the way by taking the short cut across the land. So here I am, you see, and I shall soon get to my sea-cattle!"

"Oh, what a lucky fellow you are!" exclaimed Great Claus. "Don't you think that I might have some cattle given to me, too, if I went down to the bottom of the river?"

"How can I tell?" asked Little Claus, in reply.

"You envious scoundrel! you want to keep all the beautiful sea-cattle for yourself, I warrant!" cried Great Claus. "Either you will carry me to the water's edge, and throw me over, or I will take out my great knife and kill you! Make your choice!"

"Oh no, please don't be so angry!" entreated Little Claus. "I cannot carry you in the sack to the river, you are too heavy for me; but if you will walk there yourself, and then creep into the sack, I will throw you over with all the pleasure in the world!"

134

"But if, when I get to the bottom, I find no sea-cattle for me, I shall kill you all the same when I come back, remember that!" said Great Claus; and to this arrangement Little Claus made no objection.

They walked together to the river. As soon as the thirsty cattle saw the water, they ran on as fast as they could, eagerly crowding against each other, and all wanting to drink first.

"Only look at my sea-cattle!" said Little Claus; "see how they are longing to be at the bottom of the river."

"That's all very well," said Great Claus, "but you must help me first." And he quickly crept into the great sack which had lain stretched across the shoulders of one of the oxen. "Put a heavy stone in with me," said Great Claus, "else, perhaps, I shall not sink to the bottom."

"No fear of that!" replied Little Claus. However, he put a large stone into the sack, tied the strings, and pushed the sack into the water—plump! there it fell, straight to the bottom.

"I am much afraid he will not find his sea-cattle!" observed Little Claus, and he drove his own herd quietly home to the village.

THE LITTLE MERMAID

FAR out in the wide sea,—where the water is blue as the loveliest cornflower, and clear as the purest crystal, where it is so deep that very, very many church-towers must be heaped one upon another, in order to reach from the lowest depth to the surface above,—dwell the Mer-people.

Now you must not imagine that there is nothing but sand below the water: no, indeed, far from it! Trees and plants of wondrous beauty grow there, whose stems and leaves are so light, that they are waved to and fro by the slightest motion of the water, almost as if they were living beings. Fishes, great and small, glide in and out among the branches, just as birds fly about among our trees.

Where the water is deepest, stands the palace of the Mer-king. The walls of this palace are of coral, and the high, pointed windows are of amber; the roof, however, is composed of mussel-shells, which, as the billows pass over them, are continually opening and shutting. This looks exceedingly pretty, especially as each of these mussel-shells contains a number of bright, glittering pearls, one only of which would be the most costly ornament in the diadem of a king in the upper world.

The Mer-king, who lived in this palace, had been for many years a widower; his old mother managed the household affairs for him. She was, on the whole, a sensible sort of a lady, although extremely proud of her high birth and station, on which account she wore twelve oysters on her tail, whilst the other inhabitants of the sea, even those of distinction, were allowed only six. In every other respect she merited unlimited praise, especially for the affection she showed to the six little princesses, her grand-daughters. These were all very beautiful children; the youngest was, however, the most lovely; her skin was as soft and delicate as a rose-petal, her eyes were of as deep a blue as the sea, but like all other mermaids, she had no feet; her body ended in a tail like that of a fish.

The whole day long the children used to play in the spacious apart-ments of the palace, where beautiful flowers grew out of the walls on all sides around them. When the great amber windows were opened, fishes would swim into these apartments as swallows fly into our rooms; but the fishes were bolder than the swallows; they swam straight up to the little princesses, ate from their hands, and allowed themselves to be caressed.

In front of the palace there was a large garden, full of fiery red and dark blue trees, whose fruit glittered like gold, and whose flowers resembled a bright, burning sun. The sand that formed the soil of the garden was of a bright blue colour, something like flames of sulphur; and a strangely beautiful blue was spread over the whole, so that one might have fancied oneself raised very high in the air, with the sky at once above and below, certainly not at the bottom of the sea. When the waters were quite still the sun might be seen looking like a purple flower, out of whose cup streamed forth the light of the world.

Each of the little princesses had her own plot in the garden, where she might plant and sow at her pleasure. One chose hers to be made in the shape of a whale, another preferred the figure of a mermaid, but the youngest had hers quite round like the sun, and planted in it only those flowers that were red, as the sun seemed to her. She was certainly a singular child, very quiet and thoughtful. Whilst her sisters were adorning themselves with all sorts of gay things that came out of a ship which had been wrecked, she asked for nothing but a beautiful white marble statue of a boy, which had been found in it. She put the statue in her garden, and planted a red weeping willow by its side. The tree grew up quickly, and let its long boughs fall upon the bright blue ground, where ever-moving shadows played in violet hues, as if boughs and root were embracing.

Nothing pleased the little princess more than to hear about the world of human beings living above the sea. She made her old grandmother tell her everything she knew about ships, towns, men, and land animals, and was particularly pleased when she heard that the flowers of the upper world had a pleasant fragrance (for the flowers of the sea are scentless), and that the woods were green, and the fishes fluttering among the branches of various gay colours, and that they could sing with a loud clear voice. The old lady meant birds, but she called them fishes, because her grandchildren, having never seen a bird, would not otherwise have understood her.

"When you have attained your fifteenth year," added she, "you will be permitted to rise to the surface of the sea; you will then sit by moonlight in the clefts of the rocks, see the ships sail by, and learn to distinguish towns and men."

The next year the eldest of the sisters reached this happy age, but the others—alas! the second sister was a year younger than the eldest, the third a year younger than the second, and so on; the youngest had still five whole years to wait till that joyful time should come when she also might rise to the surface of the water and see what was going on in the upper world; however, the eldest promised to tell the others of everything she might see, when the first day of her being of age arrived; for the grandmother gave them but little information, and there was so much that they wished to hear.

But none of all the sisters longed so ardently for the day when she should be released from childish restraint as the youngest: she who had longest to wait, and was so quiet and thoughtful. Many a night she stood by the open window, looking up through the clear blue water, whilst the fishes were leaping and playing around her. She could see the sun and the moon; their light was pale, but they appeared larger than they do to those who live in the upper world. If a shadow passed over them, she knew it must be either a whale or a ship sailing by full of human beings, who indeed little thought that, far beneath them, a little mermaiden was passionately stretching forth her white hands towards their ship's keel.

The day had now arrived when the eldest princess had attained her fifteenth year, and was therefore allowed to rise up to the surface of the sea.

When she returned she had a thousand things to relate. Her chief pleasure had been to sit upon a sandbank in the moonlight, looking at the large town which lay on the coast, where lights were beaming like stars, and where music was playing; she had heard the distant noise of men and carriages, she had seen the high church-towers, had listened to the ringing of the bells; and just because she could not go there she longed the more after all these things.

How attentively did her youngest sister listen to her words. And when she next stood at night time, by her open window, gazing upwards through the blue waters, she thought so intensely of the great noisy city that she fancied she could hear the church-bells ringing.

Next year the second sister received permission to swim wherever she pleased. She rose to the surface of the sea, just when the sun was setting; and this sight so delighted her, that she declared it to be more beautiful than anything else she had seen above the waters.

"The whole sky seemed tinged with gold," said she, "and it is impossible for me to describe to you the beauty of the clouds. Now red, now violet, they glided over me; but still more swiftly flew over the water a flock of white swans, just where the sun was descending; I looked after them, but the sun disappeared, and the bright rosy light on the surface of the sea and on the edges of the clouds was gradually extinguished."

It was now time for the third sister to visit the upper world. She was the boldest of the six, and ventured up a river. On its shores she saw green hills covered with woods and vineyards, from among which arose houses and castles; she heard the birds singing, and the sun shone with so much power, that she was continually obliged to plunge below, in order to cool her burning face. In a little bay she met with a number of children, who were bathing and jumping about; she would have joined in their gambols, but the children fled back to land in great terror, and a little black animal barked at her in such a manner, that she herself was frightened at last, and swam back to the sea. She could not, however, forget the green woods, the verdant hills, and the pretty children, who, although they had no fins, were swimming about in the river so fearlessly.

The fourth sister was not so bold; she remained in the open sea, and said on her return home, she thought nothing could be more beautiful. She had seen ships sailing by, so far off that they looked like sea-gulls; she had watched the merry dolphins gambolling in the water, and the enormous whales, sending up into the air a thousand sparkling fountains.

The year after, the fifth sister attained her fifteenth year. Her birthday happened at a different season to that of her sisters; it was winter, the sea was of a green colour, and immense icebergs were floating on its surface. These, she said, looked like pearls; they were, however, much larger than the church-towers in the land of human beings. She sat down upon one of these pearls, and let the wind play with her long hair, but then all the ships hoisted their sails in terror and escaped as quickly as possible. In the evening the sky was covered with sails; and whilst the great mountains of ice alternately sank and rose again, and beamed with a reddish glow, flashes of lightning burst forth from the clouds, and the thunder rolled on, peal after peal. The sails of all the ships were instantly furled, and horror and fear reigned on board, but the princess sat still on the iceberg, looking unconcernedly at the blue zigzag of the flashes.

The first time that any of these sisters rose out of the sea, she was quite enchanted at the sight of so many new and beautiful objects, but the novelty was soon over, and it was not long ere their own home appeared more attractive than the upper world, for there only did they find everything agreeable.

Many an evening would the five sisters rise hand in hand from the depths of the ocean. Their voices were far sweeter than any human voice, and when a storm was coming on, they would swim in front of the ships, and sing,—oh! how sweetly did they sing!—describing the happiness of those who lived at the bottom of the sea, and entreating the sailors not to be afraid, but to come down to them.

The mariners, however, did not understand their words; they fancied the song was only the whistling of the wind, and thus they lost the hidden glories of the sea; for if their ships were wrecked, all on board were drowned, and none but dead men ever entered the Mer-king's palace.

Whilst the sisters were swimming at evening time, the youngest would remain motionless and alone, in her father's palace, looking up after them. She would have wept, but mermaids cannot weep, and therefore, when they are troubled, suffer infinitely more than human beings do.

"Oh! if I were but fifteen!" sighed she, "I know that I should love the upper world and its inhabitants so much."

At last the time she had so longed for arrived.

"Well, now, it is your turn," said the grandmother, "come here that I may adorn you like your sisters." And she wound around her hair a wreath of white lilies, whose every petal was the half of a pearl, and then commanded eight large oysters to fasten themselves to the princess's tail, in token of her high rank.

"But that is so very uncomfortable!" said the little princess.

"One must not mind slight inconveniences when one wishes to look well," said the old lady.

How willingly would the princess have given up all this splendour, and exchanged her heavy crown for the red flowers of her garden, which were so much more becoming to her. But she dared not do so. "Farewell," said she; and she rose from the sea, light as a flake of foam.

When, for the first time in her life, she appeared on the surface of the water, the sun had just sunk below the horizon, the clouds were beaming with bright golden and rosy hues, the evening star was shining in the pale western sky, the air was mild and refreshing, and the sea as smooth as a looking-glass. A large ship with three masts lay on the still waters; one sail only was unfurled, but not a breath was stirring, and the sailors were quietly seated on the cordage and ladders of the vessel. Music and song resounded from the deck, and after it grew dark hundreds of lamps all of a sudden burst forth into light, whilst innumerable flags were fluttering overhead. The little mermaid swam close up to the captain's cabin, and every now and then when the ship was raised by the motion of the water, she could look through the clear window panes. She saw within many richly dressed men; the handsomest among them was a young prince with large black eyes. He could not certainly be more than sixteen years old, and it was in honour of his birthday that a grand festival was being celebrated. The crew were dancing on the deck, and when the young prince appeared among them, a hundred rockets were sent up into the air, turning night into day, and so terrifying the little mermaid, that for some minutes she plunged beneath the water. However, she soon raised her little head again, and then it seemed as if all the stars were falling down upon her. Such a fiery shower she had never even seen before, never had she heard that men possessed such wonderful powers. Large suns revolved around her, bright fishes swam in the air, and everything was reflected perfectly on the clear surface of the sea. It was so light in the ship, that everything could be seen distinctly. Oh! how happy the young prince was! he shook hands with the sailors, laughed and jested with them, whilst sweet notes of music mingled with the silence of night.

It was now late, but the little mermaid could not tear herself away from the ship and the handsome young prince. She remained looking through the cabin window, rocked to and fro by the waves. There was a foaming and fermentation in the depths beneath, and the ship began to move on faster, the sails were spread, the waves rose high, thick clouds gathered over the sky, and the noise of distant thunder was heard. The sailors perceived that a storm was coming on, so they again furled the sails. The great vessel was tossed about on the tempestuous ocean like a light boat, and the waves rose to an immense height, towering over the ship, which alternately sank beneath and rose above them. To the little mermaid this seemed most delightful, but the ship's crew thought very differently. The vessel cracked, the stout masts bent under the violence of the billows, the waters rushed in. For a minute the ship tottered to and fro, then the mainmast broke as if it had been a reed; the ship turned over, and was filled with water. The little mermaid now perceived that the crew was in danger, for she herself was forced to beware of the beams and splinters torn from the vessel, and floating about on the waves. But at the same time it became pitch dark so that she could not distinguish anything; presently, however, a dreadful flash of lightning disclosed to her the whole of the wreck. Her eyes sought the young prince—the same instant the ship sank to the bottom. At first she was delighted, thinking that the prince must now come to her abode, but she soon remembered that man cannot live in water, and that therefore if the prince ever entered her palace, it would be as a corpse.

"Die! no, he must not die!" She swam through the fragments with which the water was strewn regardless of the danger she was incurring, and at last found the prince all but exhausted, and with great difficulty keeping his head above water. He had already closed his eyes, and must inevitably have been drowned, had not the little mermaid come to his rescue. She seized hold of him and kept him above water, suffering the current to bear them on together.

Towards morning the storm was hushed; no trace, however, remained of the ship. The sun rose like fire out of the sea; his beams seemed to restore colour to the prince's cheeks, but his eyes were still closed. The mermaid kissed his high forehead and stroked his wet hair away from his face. He looked like the marble statue in her garden; she kissed him again and wished most fervently that he might recover.

She now saw the dry land with its mountains glittering with snow. A green wood extended along the coast, and at the entrance of the wood stood a chapel or convent, she could not be sure which. Citron and lemon trees grew in the garden adjoining it, an avenue of tall palm trees led up to the door. The sea here formed a little bay, in which the water was quite smooth but very deep, and under the cliffs there were dry firm sands. Hither swam the little mermaid with the seemingly dead prince; she laid him upon the warm sand, and took care to place his head high, and to turn his face to the sun.

The bells began to ring in the large white building which stood before her, and a number of young girls came out to walk in the garden. The mermaid went away from the shore, hid herself behind some stones, covered her head with foam, so that her little face could not be seen, and watched the prince with unremitting attention.

It was not long before one of the young girls approached. She seemed quite frightened at finding the prince in this state apparently dead; soon, however, she recovered herself, and ran back to call her sisters. The little mermaid saw that the prince revived, and that all around smiled kindly and joyfully upon him—for her, however, he looked not, he knew not that it was she who had saved him, and when the prince was taken into the house, she felt so sad, that she immediately plunged beneath the water, and returned to her father's palace.

If she had been before quiet and thoughtful, she now grew still more so. Her sisters asked her what she had seen in the upper world, but she made no answer.

Many an evening she rose to the place where she had left the prince. She saw the snow on the mountains melt, the fruits in the garden ripen and gathered, but the prince she never saw, so she always returned sorrowfully to her subterranean abode. Her only pleasure was to sit in her little garden gazing on the beautiful statue so like the prince. She cared no longer for her flowers; they grew up in wild luxuriance, covered the steps, and entwined their long stems and tendrils among the boughs of the trees, so that her whole garden became a bower.

At last, being unable to conceal her sorrow any longer, she revealed the secret to one of her sisters, who told it to the other princesses, and they to some of their friends. Among them was a young mermaid who recollected the prince, having been an eye-witness herself to the festivities in the ship; she knew also in what country the prince lived, and the name of its king.

"Come, little sister!" said the princesses, and embracing her, they rose together arm in arm, out of the water, just in front of the prince's palace.

This palace was built of bright yellow stones, a flight of white marble steps led from it down to the sea. A gilded cupola crowned the building, and white marble figures, which might almost have been taken for real men and women, were placed among the pillars surrounding it. Through the clear glass of the high windows one might look into magnificent apartments hung with silken curtains, the walls adorned with magnificent paintings. It was a real treat to the little royal mermaids to behold so splendid an abode; they gazed through the windows of one of the largest rooms, and in the centre saw a fountain playing, whose waters sprang up so high as to reach the glittering cupola above, through which the sunbeams fell dancing on the water, and brightening the pretty plants which grew around it.

The little mermaid now knew where her beloved prince dwelt, and henceforth she went there almost every evening. She often approached nearer the land than her sisters had ventured, and even swam up the narrow channel that flowed under the marble balcony. Here on a bright moonlight night, she would watch the young prince who believed himself alone.

Sometimes she saw him sailing on the water in a gaily-painted boat with many coloured flags waving above. She would then hide among the green reeds which grew on the banks, listening to his voice, and if any one in the boat noticed the rustling of her long silver veil, which was caught now and then by the light breeze, they only fancied it was a swan flapping his wings.

Many a night when the fishermen were casting their nets by the beacon's light, she heard them talking of the prince, and relating the noble actions he had performed. She was then so happy, thinking how she had saved his life when struggling with the waves, and remembering how his head had rested on her bosom, and how she had kissed him when he knew nothing of it, and could never even dream of such a thing.

Human beings became more and more dear to her every day; she wished that she were one of them. Their world seemed to her much larger than that of the mer-people; they could fly over the ocean in their ships, as well as climb to the summits of those high mountains that rose above the clouds; and their wooded domains extended much farther than a mermaid's eye could penetrate.

145

Sometimes she saw him sailing on the water

There were many things that she wished to hear explained, but her sisters could not give her any satisfactory answer; she was again obliged to have recourse to the old queen-mother, who knew a great deal about the upper world, which she used to call "the country above the sea".

"Do men live for ever when they are not drowned?" she asked one day. "Do they not die as we do, who live at the bottom of the sea?"

"Yes," was the grandmother's reply, "they must die like us, and their life is much shorter than ours. We live to the age of three hundred years, but when we die, we become foam on the sea, and are not allowed even to share a grave among those that are dear to us. We have no immortal souls, we can never live again, and are like the grass which, when once cut down, is withered for ever. Human beings, on the contrary, have souls that continue to live when their bodies become dust, and as we rise out of the water to admire the abode of man, they ascend to glorious unknown dwellings in the skies which we are not permitted to see."

"Why have not *we* immortal souls?" asked the little mermaid. "I would willingly give up my three hundred years to be a human being for only one day, thus to become entitled to that heavenly world above."

"You must not think of that," answered her grandmother, "it is much better as it is; we live longer and are far happier than human beings."

"So I must die, and be dashed like foam over the sea, never to rise again and hear the gentle murmur of the ocean, never again see the beautiful flowers and the bright sun! Tell me, dear grandmother, are there no means by which I may obtain an immortal soul?"

"No!" replied the old lady. "It is true that if thou couldst so win the affections of a human being as to become dearer to him than either father or mother; if he loved thee with all his heart, and promised whilst the priest joined his hands with thine to be always faithful to thee; then his soul would flow into thine, and thou wouldst then become partaker of human bliss. But that can never be! for what in our eyes is the most beautiful part of our body, the tail, the inhabitants of the earth think hideous; they cannot bear it. To appear handsome to them, the body must have two clumsy props which they call legs."

The little mermaid sighed and looked mournfully at the scaly part of her form, otherwise so fair and delicate.

"We are happy," added the old lady, "we shall jump and swim about merrily for three hundred years; that is a long time, and afterwards we shall repose peacefully in death. This evening we have a court ball."

The ball which the queen-mother spoke of was far more splendid than any that earth has ever seen. The walls of the salon were of crystal, very thick, but yet very clear; hundreds of large mussel-shells were planted in rows along them; these shells were some of rose-colour, some green as grass, but all sending forth a bright light, which not only illuminated the whole apartment, but also shone through the glassy walls so as to light up the waters around for a great space, and making the scales of the numberless fishes, great and small, crimson and purple, silver and gold-coloured, appear more brilliant than ever.

Through the centre of the salon flowed a bright, clear stream, on the surface of which danced mermen and mermaids to the melody of their own sweet voices, voices far sweeter than those of the dwellers upon earth. The little princess sang more harmoniously than any other, and they clapped their hands and applauded her. She was pleased at this, for she knew well that there was neither on earth nor in the sea a more beautiful voice than hers. But her thoughts soon returned to the world above her; she could not forget the handsome prince; she could not control her sorrow at not having an immortal soul. She stole away from her father's palace, and whilst all was joy within, she sat alone lost in thought in her little neglected garden. On a sudden she heard the tones of horns resounding over the water far away in the distance, and she said to herself, "Now he is going out to hunt, he whom I love more than my father and my mother, with whom my thoughts are constantly occupied, and to whom I would so willingly trust the happiness of my life! All! all, will I risk to win him—and an immortal soul! Whilst my sisters are still dancing in the palace, I will go to the enchantress whom I have hitherto feared so much, but who is, nevertheless, the only person who can advise and help me."

So the little mermaid left the garden and went to the foaming whirlpool, beyond which dwelt the enchantress. She had never been this way before—neither flowers nor sea-grass bloomed along her path; she had to traverse an extent of bare grey sand till she reached the whirlpool, whose waters were eddying and whizzing like mill-wheels, tearing everything they could seize along with them into the abyss below. She was obliged to make her way through this horrible place, in order to arrive at the territory of the enchantress. Then she had to pass through a boiling, slimy bog, which the enchantress called her turf-moor: her house stood in a wood beyond this, and a strange abode it was. All the trees and bushes around were polypi, looking like hundred-headed serpents shooting up out of the ground; their branches were long slimy arms with fingers of worms, every member, from the root to the uttermost tip, ceaselessly moving and extending on all sides. Whatever they seized they fastened upon so that it could not loosen itself from their grasp. The little mermaid stood still for a minute looking at this horrible wood; her heart beat with fear, and she would certainly have returned without attaining her object, had she not remembered the prince—and immortality. The thought gave her new courage, she bound up her long waving hair, that the polypi might not catch hold of it, crossed her delicate arms over her bosom, and, swifter than a fish can glide through the water, she passed these unseemly trees, who stretched their eager arms after her in vain. She could not, however, help seeing that every polypus had something in his grasp, held as firmly by a thousand little arms as if enclosed by iron bands. The whitened skeletons of a number of human beings who had been drowned in the sea, and had sunk into the abyss, grinned horribly from the arms of these polypi; helms, chests, skeletons of land animals were also held in their embrace; among other things might be seen even a little mermaid whom they had seized and strangled! What a fearful sight for the unfortunate princess!

But she got safely through this wood of horrors, and then arrived at a slimy place, where immense, fat snails were crawling about, and in the midst of this place stood a house built of the bones of unfortunate people who had been shipwrecked. Here sat the witch caressing a toad in the same manner as some persons would a pet bird. The ugly fat snails she called her chickens, and she permitted them to crawl about her.

"I know well what you would ask of me," said she to the little princess. "Your wish is foolish enough, yet it shall be fulfilled, though its accomplishment is sure to bring misfortune on you, my fairest princess. You wish to get rid of your tail, and to have instead two stilts like those of human beings, in order that a young prince may fall in love with you, and that you may obtain an immortal soul. Is it not so?" Whilst the witch spoke these words, she laughed so violently that her pet toad and snails fell from her lap. "You come just at the right time," continued she; "had you come after sunset, it would not have been in my power to have helped you before another year. I will prepare for you a drink with which you must swim to land, you must sit down upon the shore and swallow it, and then your tail will fall and shrink up to the things which men call legs. This transformation will, however, be very painful; you will feel as though a sharp knife passed through your body. All who look on you after you have been thus changed will say that you are the loveliest child of earth they have ever seen; you will retain your peculiar undulating movements, and no dancer will move so lightly, but every step you take will cause you pain all but unbearable; it will seem to you as though you were walking on the sharp edges of swords, and your blood will flow. Can you endure all this suffering? If so, I will grant your request."

"Yes, I will," answered the princess, with a faltering voice; for she remembered her dear prince, and the immortal soul which her suffering might win.

"Only consider," said the witch, "that you can never again become a mermaid, when once you have received a human form. You may never return to your sisters, and your father's palace; and unless you shall win the prince's love to such a degree that he shall leave father and mother for you, that you shall be mixed up with all his thoughts and wishes, and unless the priest join your hands, so that you become man and wife, you will never obtain the immortality you seek. The morrow of the day on which he is united to another will see your death; your heart will break with sorrow, and you will be changed to foam on the sea."

"Still I will venture!" said the little mermaid, pale and trembling as a dying person.

"Besides all this, I must be paid, and it is no slight thing that I require for my trouble. Thou hast the sweetest voice of all the dwellers in the sea, and thou thinkest by its means to charm the prince; this voice, however, I demand as my recompense. The best thing thou possessest I require in exchange for my magic drink; for I shall be obliged to sacrifice my own blood, in order to give it the sharpness of a two-edged sword."

"But if you take my voice from me," said the princess, "what have I left with which to charm the prince?"

"The graceful form," replied the witch, "the modest gait, and speaking eyes. With such as these, it will be easy to infatuate a vain human heart. Well now! hast thou lost courage? Put out thy little tongue, that I may cut it off, and take it for myself, in return for my magic drink."

"Be it so!" said the princess, and the witch took up her cauldron, in order to mix her potion. "Cleanliness is a good thing," remarked she, as she began to rub the cauldron with a handful of toads and snails. She then scratched her bosom, and let the black blood trickle down into the cauldron, every moment throwing in new ingredients, the smoke from the mixture assuming such horrible forms as were enough to fill beholders with terror, and a moaning and groaning proceeding from it, which might be compared to the weeping of crocodiles. The magic drink at length became clear and transparent as pure water; it was ready.

"Here it is!" said the witch to the princess, cutting out her tongue at the same moment. The poor little mermaid was now dumb: she could neither sing nor speak.

"If the polypi should attempt to seize you, as you pass through my little grove," said the witch, "you have only to sprinkle some of this magic drink over them, and their arms will burst into a thousand pieces." But the princess had no need of this counsel, for the polypi drew hastily back, as soon as they perceived the bright phial that glittered in her hand like a star; thus she passed safely through the formidable wood over the moor, and across the foaming mill-stream.

She now looked once again at her father's palace; the lamps in the salon were extinguished, and all the family were asleep. She would not go in, for she could not speak if she did; she was about to leave her home for ever; her heart was ready to break with sorrow at the thought; she stole into the garden, plucked a flower from the bed of each of her sisters as a remembrance, kissed her hand to them again and again, and then rose through the dark blue waters to the world above.

The sun had not yet risen when she arrived at the prince's dwelling, and ascended those well-known marble steps. The moon still shone in the sky when the little mermaid drank the wonderful liquid contained in her phial—she felt it run through her like a sharp knife, and she fell down in a swoon. When the sun rose, she awoke, and felt a burning pain in all her limbs, but—she saw standing close to her the object of her love, the handsome young prince, whose coal-black eyes were fixed inquiringly upon her. Full of shame she cast down her own, and perceived, instead of the long fish-like tail she had hitherto borne, two slender legs; but she was quite naked, and tried in vain to cover herself with her long thick hair. The prince asked who she was, and how she had got there; and she, in reply, smiled and gazed upon him with her bright blue eyes, for alas! she could not speak. He then led her by the hand into the palace. She found that the witch had told her true; she felt as though she were walking on the edges of sharp swords, but she bore the pain willingly; on she passed, light as a zephyr, and all who saw her wondered at her light undulating movements.

When she entered the palace, rich clothes of muslin and silk were brought to her; she was lovelier than all who dwelt there, but she could neither speak nor sing. Some female slaves, gaily dressed in silk and gold brocade, sang before the prince and his royal parents; and one of them distinguished herself by her clear sweet voice, which the prince applauded by clapping his hands. This made the little mermaid very sad, for she knew that she used to sing far better than the young slave. "Alas!" thought she, "if he did but know that, for his sake, I have given away my voice for ever."

The slaves began to dance; our lovely little mermaiden then arose, stretched out her delicate white arms, and hovered gracefully about the room. Every motion displayed more and more the perfect symmetry and elegance of her figure; and the expression which beamed in her speaking eyes touched the hearts of the spectators far more than the song of the slaves.

All present were enchanted, but especially the young prince, who called her his dear little foundling. And she danced again and again, although every step cost her excessive pain. The prince then said she should always be with him; and accordingly a sleeping place was prepared for her on velvet cushions in the anteroom of his own apartment.

The prince caused a suit of riding apparel to be made for her, in order that she might accompany him in his rides; so together they traversed the fragrant woods, where green boughs brushed against their shoulders, and the birds sang merrily among the fresh leaves. With him she climbed up steep mountains, and although her tender feet bled, so as to be remarked by the attendants, she only smiled, and followed her dear prince to the heights, whence they could see the clouds chasing each other beneath them, like a flock of birds migrating to other countries.

During the night she would, when all in the palace were at rest, walk down the marble steps, in order to cool her feet in the deep waters; she would then think of those beloved ones who dwelt in the lower world.

One night, as she was thus bathing her feet, her sisters swam together to the spot, arm in arm and singing, but alas! so mournfully! She beckoned to them, and they immediately recognised her, and told her how great was the mourning in her father's house for her loss. From this time the sisters visited her every night; and once they brought with them the old grandmother, who had not seen the upper world for a great many years; they likewise brought their father, the Mer-king, with his crown on his head; but these two old people did not venture near enough to land to be able to speak to her.

The little mermaiden became dearer and dearer to the prince every day; but he only looked upon her as a sweet, gentle child; and the thought of making her his wife never entered his head. And yet his wife she must be, ere she could receive an immortal soul; his wife she must be, or she would change into foam, and be driven restlessly over the billows of the sea!

"Dost thou not love me above all others?" her eyes seemed to ask, as he pressed her fondly in his arms, and kissed her lovely brow.

"Yes," the prince would say, "thou art dearer to me than any other, for no one is as good as thou art! Thou lovest me so much; and thou art so like a young maiden, whom I have seen but once, and may never see again. I was on board a ship, which was wrecked by a sudden tempest; the waves threw me on the shore, near a holy temple, where a number of young girls are occupied constantly with religious services. The youngest of them found me on the shore, and saved my life. I saw her only once, but her image is vividly impressed upon my memory, and her alone can I love. But she belongs to the holy temple; and thou who resemblest her so much hast been given to me for consolation; never will we be parted!"

"Alas! he does not know that it was I who saved his life," thought the little mermaiden, sighing deeply; "I bore him over the wild waves, into the wooded bay, where the holy temple stood; I sat behind the rocks, waiting till some one should come. I saw the pretty maiden approach, whom he loves more than me,"—and again she heaved a deep sigh, for she could not weep,—"he said that the young girl belongs to the holy temple; she never comes out into the world, so they cannot meet each other again—and I am always with him, and see him daily; I will love him, and devote my whole life to him."

"So the prince is going to be married to the beautiful daughter of the neighbouring king," said the courtiers, "that is why he is having that splendid ship fitted out. It is announced that he wishes to travel, but in reality he goes to see the princess; a numerous retinue will accompany him." The little mermaiden smiled at these and similar conjectures, for she knew the prince's intentions better than any one else.

"I must go," he said to her, "I must see the beautiful princess; my parents require me to do so; but they will not compel me to marry her, and bring her home as my bride. And it is quite impossible for me to love her, for she cannot be so like the beautiful girl in the temple as thou art; and if I were obliged to choose, I should prefer thee, my little silent foundling, with the speaking eyes." And he kissed her rosy lips, played with her locks, and folded her in his arms, whereupon arose in her heart a sweet vision of human happiness, and immortal bliss.

"Thou art not afraid of the sea, art thou, my sweet silent child?" asked he tenderly, as they stood together in the splendid ship, which was to take them to the country of the neighbouring king. And then he told her of the storms that sometimes agitate the waters; of the strange fishes that inhabit the deep, and of the wonderful things seen by divers. But she smiled at his words, for she knew better than any child of earth what went on in the depths of the ocean.

At night time, when the moon shone brightly, and when all on board were fast asleep, she sat in the ship's gallery, looking down into the sea. It seemed to her, as she gazed through the foamy track made by the ship's keel, that she saw her father's palace, and her grandmother's silver crown. She then saw her sisters rise out of the water, looking sorrowful and stretching out their hands towards her. She nodded to them, smiled, and would have explained that everything was going on quite according to her wishes; but just then the cabin boy approached, upon which the sisters plunged beneath the water so suddenly that the boy thought what he had seen on the waves was nothing but foam.

The next morning the ship entered the harbour of the king's splendid capital. Bells were rung, trumpets sounded, and soldiers marched in procession through the city, with waving banners, and glittering bayonets. Every day witnessed some new entertainments, balls and parties followed each other; the princess, however, was not yet in the town; she had been sent to a distant convent for education, and had there been taught the practice of all royal virtues. At last she arrived at the palace.

The little mermaid had been anxious to see this unparalleled princess; and she was now obliged to confess that she had never before seen so beautiful a creature.

The skin of the princess was so white and delicate, that the veins might be seen through it, and her dark eyes sparkled beneath a pair of finely formed eyebrows.

"It is herself!" exclaimed the prince, when they met; "it is she who saved my life, when I lay like a corpse on the seashore!" and he pressed his blushing bride to his beating heart.

"Oh, I am all too happy!" said he to his dumb foundling. "What I never dared to hope for has come to pass. Thou must rejoice in my happiness, for thou lovest me more than all others who surround me." And the little mermaid kissed his hand in silent sorrow; it seemed to her as if her heart was breaking already, although the morrow of his marriage day, which must inevitably see her death, had not yet dawned.

Again rang the church-bells, whilst heralds rode through the streets of the capital, to announce the approaching wedding. Flames burned in silver candlesticks on all the altars; the priests swung their golden censers; and the bride and bridegroom joined hands, whilst the holy words that united them were spoken. The little mermaid, clad in silk and cloth of gold, stood behind the princess, and held the train of the bridal dress; but her ear heard nothing of the solemn music; her eye saw not the holy ceremony; she remembered her approaching end, she remembered that she had lost both this world and the next.

That very same evening, bride and bridegroom went on board the ship; cannons were fired, flags waved with the breeze, and in the centre of the deck stood a magnificent pavilion of purple and cloth of gold, fitted up with the richest and softest couches. Here the princely pair were to spend the night. A favourable wind swelled the sails, and the ship glided lightly over the blue waters.

As soon as it was dark, coloured lamps were hung out and dancing began on the deck. The little mermaid was thus involuntarily reminded of what she had seen the first time she rose to the upper world. The spectacle that now presented itself was equally splendid —and she was obliged to join in the dance, hovering lightly as a bird over the ship boards. All applauded her, for never had she danced with more enchanting grace. Her little feet suffered extremely, but she no longer felt the pain; the anguish her heart suffered was much greater. It was the last evening she might see him, for whose sake she had forsaken her home and all her family, had given away her beautiful voice, and suffered daily the most violent pain—all without his having the least suspicion of it. It was the last evening that she might breathe the same atmosphere in which he, the beloved one, lived; the last evening when she might behold the deep blue sea, and the starry heavens—an eternal night, in which she might neither think nor dream, awaited her. And all was joy in the ship; and she, her heart filled with thoughts of death and annihilation, smiled and danced with the others, till past midnight. Then the prince kissed his lovely bride, and arm in arm they entered the magnificent tent, prepared for their repose.

All was now still; the steersman alone stood at the ship's helm. The little mermaid leaned her white arms on the gallery, and looked towards the east, watching for the dawn; she well knew that the first sunbeam would witness her dissolution. She saw her sisters rise out of the sea; deadly pale were their features, and their long hair no more fluttered over their shoulders, it had all been cut off.

"We have given it to the witch," said they, "to induce her to help thee, so that thou mayest not die. She has given to us a knife: here it is! before the sun rises, thou must plunge it into the prince's heart; and when his warm blood trickles down upon thy feet they will again be changed to a fish-like tail; thou wilt once more become a mermaid, and wilt live thy full three hundred years, ere thou changest to foam on the sea. But hasten! either he or thou must die before sunrise. Our aged mother mourns for thee so much, her grey hair has fallen off through sorrow, as ours fell before the scissors of the witch. Kill the prince, and come down to us! hasten! hasten! dost thou not see the red streaks on the eastern sky, announcing the near approach of the sun? A few minutes more and he rises, and then all will be over with thee." At these words they sighed deeply and vanished.

The little mermaid drew aside the purple curtains of the pavilion,

158

where lay the bride and bridegroom; bending over them, she kissed the prince's forehead, and then glancing at the sky, she saw that the dawning light became every moment brighter. The prince's lips unconsciously murmured the name of his bride—he was dreaming of her, and her only, whilst the fatal knife trembled in the hand of the unhappy mermaid. All at once, she threw far out into the sea that instrument of death; the waves rose like bright blazing flames around, and the water where it fell seemed tinged with blood. With eyes fast becoming dim and fixed, she looked once more at her beloved prince; then plunged from the ship into the sea, and felt her body slowly but surely dissolving into foam.

The sun rose from his watery bed; his beams fell so softly and warmly upon her, that our little mermaid was scarcely sensible of dying. She still saw the glorious sun; and over her head hovered a thousand beautiful, transparent forms; she could still distinguish the white sails of the ship, and the bright red clouds in the sky; the voices of those airy creatures above her had a melody so sweet and soothing that a human ear would be as little able to catch the sound as her eye was capable of distinguishing their forms; they hovered around her without wings, borne by their own lightness through the air. The little mermaid at last saw that she had a body as transparent as theirs; and felt herself raised gradually from the foam of the sea to higher regions.

"Where are they taking me?" asked she, and her words sounded just like the voices of those heavenly beings.

"Speak you to the daughters of air?" was the answer. "The mermaid has no immortal soul, and can only acquire that heavenly gift by winning the love of one of the sons of men; her immortality depends upon union with man. Neither do the daughters of air possess immortal souls, but they can acquire them by their own good deeds. We fly to hot countries, where the children of earth are sinking under sultry pestilential breezes—our fresh cooling breath revives them. We diffuse ourselves through the atmosphere; we perfume it with the delicious fragrance of flowers; and thus spread delight and health over the earth. By doing good in this manner for three hundred years, we win immortality, and receive a share of the eternal bliss of human beings. And thou, poor little mermaid! who, following the impulse of thine own heart, hast done and suffered so much, thou art now raised to the airy world of spirits, that by performing deeds of kindness for three hundred years, thou mayest acquire an immortal soul."

The little mermaid stretched out her transparent arms to the sun; and, for the first time in her life, tears moistened her eyes.

And now again all were awake and rejoicing in the ship; she saw the prince, with his pretty bride; they had missed her; they looked sorrowfully down on the foamy waters, as if they knew she had plunged into the sea; unseen she kissed the bridegroom's forehead, smiled upon him, and then, with the rest of the children of air, soared high above the rosy cloud which was sailing so peacefully over the ship.

"After three hundred years we shall fly in the kingdom of Heaven!"

"We may arrive there even sooner," whispered one of her sisters. "We fly invisibly through the dwellings of men, where there are children; and whenever we find a good child, who gives pleasure to his parents and deserves their love, the good God shortens our time of probation. No child is aware that we are flitting about his room; and that whenever joy draws from us a smile, a year is struck out of our three hundred. But when we see a rude naughty child, we weep bitter tears of sorrow, and every tear we shed adds a day to our time of probation."

The little lady stretched out both her arms

THE CONSTANT TIN SOLDIER

THERE were once five-and-twenty tin soldiers, all brothers, for they had all been made out of one old tin spoon. They carried muskets in their hands, and held themselves very upright, and their uniforms were red and blue—very gay indeed. The first word that they heard in this world, when the lid was taken off the box wherein they lay, was "Tin soldiers!" It was a little boy who made this exclamation, clapping his hands at the same time. They had been given to him because it was his birthday, and he now set them out on the table. The soldiers resembled each other to a hair, one only was rather different from the rest; he had but one leg, for he had been made last, when there was not quite tin enough left; however, he stood as firmly upon his one leg as the others did upon their two; and this identical tin soldier it is whose fortunes seem to us worthy of record.

On the table where the tin soldiers were set out were several other playthings, but the most charming of them all was a pretty paste-board castle. Through its little windows one could look into the rooms. In front of the castle stood some tiny trees, clustering round a little mirror intended to represent a lake, and waxen swans swam in the lake and were reflected on its surface. All this was very pretty, but prettiest of all was a little damsel standing in the open door-way of the castle; she, too, was cut out of pasteboard, but she had on a frock of the clearest muslin, a little sky-blue riband was flung across her shoulders like a scarf, and in the midst of this scarf was set a bright gold wing. The little lady stretched out both her arms, for she was a dancer, and raised one of her legs so high in the air that the tin soldier could not find it, and fancied that she had, like him, only one leg.

"That would be just the wife for me," thought he, "but then, she is of rather too high rank; she lives in a castle. I have only a box, besides, there are all our five-and-twenty men in it; it is no place for her! However, there will be no harm in my making acquaintance with her," and so he stationed himself behind a snuff-box that stood on the table; from this place he had a full view of the delicate little lady, who still remained standing on one leg, yet without losing her balance.

When evening came, all the other tin soldiers were put away into the box, and the people of the house went to bed. The playthings now began to play in their turn; they pretended to visit, to fight battles, and give balls. The tin soldiers rattled in the box, for they wanted to play too, but the lid would not come off. The nut-crackers cut capers, and the slate-pencil played at commerce on the slate; there was such a racket that the canary bird waked up, and began to talk, too, but he always talked in verse. The only two who did not move from their places were the tin soldier and the little dancer; she constantly remained in her graceful position, standing on the point of her foot, with outstretched arms; and, as for him, he stood just as firmly on his one leg, never for one moment turning his eyes away from her.

Twelve o'clock struck. Crash! Open sprang the lid of the snuff-box, but there was no snuff inside it! no, out jumped a little black conjuror, in fact it was a Jack-in-the-box. "Tin soldier!" said the conjuror, "wilt thou keep thine eyes to thyself?"

But the tin soldier pretended not to hear.

"Well, only wait till to-morrow!" quoth the conjuror.

"When the morrow had came, and the children were out of bed, the tin soldier was placed on the window-ledge, and, whether the conjuror or the wind occasioned it, all at once the window flew open, and out fell the tin soldier, head foremost, from the third storey to the ground. A dreadful fall was that! His one leg turned over and over in the air, and at last he rested, poised on his soldier's cap, with his bayonet between two paving-stones.

The maid-servant and the little boy immediately came down to look for him; but although they very nearly trod on him, they could not see him. If the tin soldier had but called out "Here I am!" they

. . . and out fell the tin soldier, head foremost

might easily have found him; but he thought it would not be becoming for him to cry out, as he was in uniform.

It now began to rain; every drop fell heavier than the last; there was a regular shower. When it was over, two boys came by. "Look," said one, "here is a tin soldier, he shall have a sail for once in his life."

So they made a boat out of an old newspaper, put the tin soldier into it, and away he sailed down the gutter, both the boys running along by the side and clapping their hands. The paper boat rocked to and fro, and every now and then veered round so quickly that the tin soldier became quite giddy; still he moved not a muscle, looked straight before him, and held his bayonet tightly clasped.

All at once the boat sailed under a long gutter-board; he found it as dark here as at home in his own box.

"Where shall I get to next?" thought he; "yes, to be sure, it is all that conjuror's doing! Ah, if the little maiden were but sailing with me in the boat I would not care for its being twice as dark!"

Just then a great water-rat that lived under the gutter-board darted out.

"Have you a passport?" asked the rat. "Where is your passport?"

But the tin soldier was silent, and held his weapon with a still firmer grasp. The boat sailed on, and the rat followed. Oh! how furiously he showed his teeth, and cried out to sticks and straws, "Stop him, stop him! he has not paid the toll, he has not shown his passport!" But the stream grew stronger and stronger. The tin soldier could already catch a glimpse of the bright daylight before the boat came from under the tunnel, but at the same time he heard a roaring noise, at which the boldest heart might well have trembled. Only fancy! where the tunnel ended, the water of the gutter fell perpendicularly into a great canal; this was as dangerous for the tin soldier as sailing down a mighty waterfall would be for us.

He was now so close that he could no longer stand upright; the boat darted forwards, the poor tin soldier held himself as stiff and immovable as possible, no one could accuse him of having even blinked. The boat spun round and round three, nay, four times, and was filled with water to the brim; it must sink. The tin soldier stood up to his neck in water, deeper and deeper sank the boat, softer and softer grew the paper; the water went over the soldier's head, he thought of the pretty little dancer whom he should never see again, and these words rang in his ears:

> "Wild adventure, mortal danger,
> Be thy portion, valiant stranger!"

The paper now tore asunder, the tin soldier fell through the rent; but, in the same moment, he was swallowed up by a large fish. Oh, how dark it was! worse even than under the gutter-board, and so narrow, too! but the tin soldier's resolution was as constant as ever; there he lay, at full length, shouldering his arms.

The fish turned and twisted about, and made the strangest movements. At last he became quite still; a flash of lightning, as it were, darted through him. The daylight shone brightly, and some one exclaimed, "Tin soldier!" The fish had been caught, taken to the market, sold, and brought home into the kitchen, where the servant-girl was cutting him up with a large knife. She seized the tin soldier by the middle with two of her fingers, and took him into the parlour, where every one was eager to see the wonderful man who had travelled in the maw of a fish; however, our little warrior was by no means proud. They set him on the table, and there—no, how could anything so extraordinary happen in this world?—the tin soldier was in the very same room in which he had been before; he saw the same children, the same playthings stood on the table, among them the beautiful castle with the pretty little dancing maiden, who was still standing upon one leg, whilst she held the other high in the air; she too was constant. It quite affected the tin soldier; he could have found it in his heart to weep tin tears, but such weakness would have been unbecoming in a soldier. He looked at her and she looked at him, but neither of them spoke a word.

And now one of the little boys took the soldier and threw him without ceremony into the stove. He did not give any reason for so doing, but no doubt the conjuror in the snuff-box must have had a hand in it.

The tin soldier now stood in a blaze of red light; he felt extremely hot. Whether this heat were the result of the actual fire or of the flames of love within him, he knew not. He had entirely lost his colour. Whether this change had happened during his travels, or were the effect of strong emotion, I know not. He looked upon the little damsel, she looked upon him, and he felt that he was melting; but, constant as ever, he still stood shouldering his arms. A door opened, the wind seized the dancer, and, like a sylph, she flew straightway into the stove, to the tin soldier; they both flamed up into a blaze, and were gone. The soldier was melted to a hard lump, and when the maid took out the ashes the next day she found his remains in the shape of a little tin heart; of the dancer there remained only the gold wing, and that was burnt black as coal.

THE SHEPHERDESS AND THE
CHIMNEY-SWEEPER

HAVE you never seen an old-fashioned oaken-wood cabinet, quite black with age and covered with varnish and carving work? Just such a piece of furniture, an old heir-loom that had been the property of its present mistress's great-grandmother, once stood in a parlour. It was carved from top to bottom—roses, tulips, and little stags' heads with long, branching antlers, peering forth from the curious scrolls and foliage surrounding them. Moreover, in the centre panel of the cabinet was carved the full-length figure of a man, who seemed to be perpetually grinning, perhaps at himself, for in truth he was a most ridiculous figure; he had crooked legs, small horns on his forehead, and a long beard. The children of the house used to call him "the crooked-legged Field-marshal-Major-General-Corporal-Sergeant", for this was a long, hard name, and not many figures, whether carved in wood or in stone, could boast of such a title. There he stood, his eyes always fixed upon the table under the pier-glass, for on this table stood a pretty little porcelain shepherdess, her mantle gathered gracefully round her, and fastened with a red rose; her shoes and hat were gilt, her hand held a crook—oh, she was charming! Close by her stood a little chimney-sweeper, likewise of porcelain. He was as clean and neat as any of the other figures, indeed, the manufacturer might just as well have made a prince as a chimney-sweeper of him, for though elsewhere black as a coal, his face was as fresh and rosy as a girl's, which was certainly a mistake,—it ought to have been black. His ladder in his hand, there he kept his station, close by the little shepherdess; they had been placed together from the first, had always remained on the same spot, and had thus plighted their troth to each other; they suited each other so well, they were both young people, both of the same kind of porcelain, both alike fragile and delicate.

Not far off stood a figure three times as large as the others. It was an old Chinese mandarin who could nod his head; he too was of porcelain, and declared that he was grandfather to the little shepherdess. He could not prove his assertion; however, he insisted that he had authority over her, and so, when "the crooked-legged Field-marshal-Major-General-Corporal-Sergeant" made proposals to the little shepherdess, he nodded his head in token of his consent.

"Now, you will have a husband," said the old mandarin to her, "a husband who, I verily believe, is of mahogany wood; you will be the wife of a Field-marshal-Major-General-Corporal-Sergeant, of a man who has a whole cabinet full of silver plate, besides a store of of no one knows what in the secret drawers!"

"I will not go into that dismal cabinet!" declared the little shepherdess. "I have heard say that eleven porcelain ladies are already imprisoned there."

167

"Then you shall be the twelfth, and you will be in good company!" rejoined the mandarin. "This very night, when the old cabinet creaks, your nuptials shall be celebrated, as sure as I am a Chinese mandarin!"

Whereupon he nodded his head and fell asleep.

But the little shepherdess wept, and turned to the beloved of her heart, the porcelain chimney-sweep.

"I believe I must ask you," said she, "to go out with me into the wide world, for here we cannot stay."

"I will do everything you wish," replied the little chimney-sweeper; "let us go at once. I think I can support you by my profession."

"If you could but get off the table!" sighed she; "I shall never be happy till we are away, out in the wide world."

And he comforted her, and showed her how to set her little foot on the carved edges and gilded foliage twining round the leg of the table, till at last they reached the floor. But turning to look at the old cabinet, they saw everything in a grand commotion, all the carved stags putting their little heads farther out, raising their antlers, and moving their throats, whilst the crooked-legged Field-marshal-Major-General-Corporal-Sergeant sprang up, and shouted out to the old Chinese mandarin, "Look, they are eloping! they are eloping!" They were not a little frightened, and quickly jumped into an open drawer for protection.

In this drawer there were three or four incomplete packs of cards, and also a little puppet-theatre; a play was being performed, and all the queens, whether of diamonds, hearts, clubs or spades, sat in the front row fanning themselves with the flowers they held in their hands; behind them stood the knaves, showing that they had each two heads, one above and one below, as most cards have. The play was about two persons who were crossed in love, and the sherpherdess wept over it, for it was just like her own history.

"I cannot bear this!" said she. "Let us leave the drawer." But when they had again reached the floor, on looking up at the table, they saw that the old Chinese mandarin had awakened, and was rocking his whole body to and fro with rage.

"Oh, the old mandarin is coming!" cried the little shepherdess, and down she fell on her porcelain knees in the greatest distress. "A sudden thought has struck me," said the chimney-sweeper, "suppose we creep into the large pot-pourri vase that stands in the corner: there we can rest upon roses and lavender, and throw salt in his eyes if he comes near us."

"That will not do at all," said she: "besides, I know that the old mandarin was once betrothed to the pot-pourri vase, and no doubt there is still some slight friendship existing between them. No, there is no help for it, we must wander forth together into the wide world."

"Hast thou indeed the courage to go with me into the wide world?" asked the chimney-sweeper. "Hast thou considered how large it is, and that we may never return home again?"

"I have," replied she.

And the chimney-sweeper looked keenly at her, and then said, "My path leads through the chimney; hast thou indeed the courage to creep with me through the stove, through the flues and the tunnel? Well do I know the way! We shall mount up so high that they cannot come near us, and at the top there is a cavern that leads into the wide world."

And he led her to the door of the stove.

"Oh, how black it looks!" sighed she; however, she went on with him, through the flues and through the tunnel, where it was dark, pitch dark.

"Now we are in the chimney," said he; "and look, what a lovely star shines above us!"

And there was actually a star in the sky, shining right down upon them, as if to show them the way. And they crawled and crept—a fearful path was theirs—so high, so very high! but he guided and supported her, and showed her the best places whereon to plant her tiny porcelain feet, till they reached the edge of the chimney, where they sat down to rest, for they were very tired, and indeed not without reason.

Heaven with all its stars was above them, and the town with all its roofs lay beneath them; the wide, wide world surrounded them. The poor shepherdess had never imagined all this; she leant her little head on her chimney-sweeper's arm, and wept so vehemently that the gilding broke off from her waistband.

"This is too much!" exclaimed she. "This can I not endure! The world is all too large! Oh that I were once more upon the little table under the pier-glass! I shall never be happy till I am there again. I have followed thee out into the wide world, surely thou canst follow me home again, if thou lovest me!"

And the chimney-sweeper talked very sensibly to her, reminding her of the old Chinese mandarin and "the crooked-legged Field-marshal-Major-Corporal-Sergeant", but she wept so bitterly, and kissed her little chimney-sweep so fondly, that at last he could not but yield to her request, unreasonable as it was.

So with great difficulty they crawled down the chimney, crept through the flues and the tunnel, and at length found themselves once more in the dark stove; but they still lurked behind the door, listening, before they would venture to return into the room. Everything was quite still; they peeped out: oh dear, on the ground lay the old Chinese mandarin! In attempting to follow the runaways, he had fallen down off the table and had broken into three pieces; his head lay shaking in a corner; "the crooked-legged Field-marshal-Major-General-Corporal-Sergeant" stood where he had always stood, thinking over what had happened.

"Oh, how shocking!" exclaimed the little shepherdess, "old grand-father is broken in pieces, and we are the cause! I shall never survive it!" and she wrung her delicate hands.

"He can be put together again," replied the chimney-sweeper. "He can very easily be put together; only be not so impatient! If they glue his back together, and put a strong rivet in his neck, then he will be as good as new again, and will be able to say plenty of unpleasant things to us."

"Do you really think so?" asked she. And then they climbed up the table to the place where they had stood before.

"See how far we have been!" observed the chimney-sweeper, "we might have spared ourselves all the trouble."

"If we could but have old grandfather put together!" said the shepherdess. "Will it cost very much?"

And he was put together; the family had his back glued and his neck riveted; he was as good as new, but could no longer nod his head.

"You have certainly grown very proud since you broke in pieces!" remarked the crooked-legged Field-marshal-Major-General-Corporal-Sergeant, "but I must say, for my part, I do not see that there is anything to be proud of. Am I to have her or am I not? Just answer me that!"

And the chimney-sweeper and the little shepherdess looked imploringly at the old mandarin; they were so afraid lest he should nod his head, but nod he could not, and it was disagreeable to him to tell a stranger that he had a rivet in his neck, so the young porcelain people always remained together, they blessed the grandfather's rivet, and loved each other till they broke in pieces.

THE TINDER BOX

A SOLDIER was marching along the high-road—right, left! right, left! He had his knapsack on his back and a sword by his side, for he had been to the wars, and was now returning home. And on the road he met an old witch; a horrid-looking creature she was, her lower lip hung down almost to her neck.

"Good evening, soldier!" she she. "What a bright sword, and what a large knapsack you have, my fine fellow! I'll tell you what; you shall have as much money for your own as you can wish!"

"Thanks, old witch!" cried the soldier.

"Do you see yonder large tree?" said the witch, pointing to a tree that stood close by the wayside. "It is quite hollow within. Climb up to the top, and you will find a hole large enough for you to creep through, and thus you will get down into the tree. I will tie a rope round your waist, so that I can pull you up again when you call me."

"But what am I to do down in the tree?" asked the soldier.

"What are you to do?" repeated the witch; "why, fetch money, to be sure! As soon as you get to the bottom, you will find yourself in a wide passage; it is quite light, more than a hundred lamps are burning there. Then you will see three doors; you can open them, the keys are in the locks. On opening the first door you will enter a room. In the midst of it, on the floor, lies a large chest; a dog is seated on it, his eyes are as large as tea-cups; but never you mind, don't trouble yourself about him! I will lend you my blue apron; you must spread it out on the floor, then go briskly up to the dog, seize him, and set him down on it; and after that is done, you can open the chest, and take as much money out of it as you please. That chest contains none but copper coins; but if you like silver better, you have only to go into the next room; there you will find a dog with eyes as large as mill-wheels, but don't be afraid of him; you have only to set him down on my apron, and then rifle the chest at your leisure. But if you would rather have gold than either silver or copper, that is to be had too, and as much of it as you can carry, if you pass on into the third chamber. The dog that sits on this third money-chest has two eyes, each as large as the Round Tower. A famous creature he is, as you may fancy; but don't be alarmed, just set him down on my apron, and then he will do you no harm, and you can take as much golden treasure from the chest as you like."

"Not a bad plan that, upon my word!" said the soldier. "But how

A real Princess was this!

much of the money am I to give you, old woman? For you'll want your full share of the plunder, I've a notion!"

"Not a penny will I have," returned the witch. "The only thing I want you to bring me is an old tinder-box which my grandmother left there by mistake last time she was down in the tree."

"Well then, give me the rope to tie round my waist, and I'll be gone," said the soldier.

"Here it is," said the witch, "and here is my blue apron."

So the soldier climbed the tree, let himself down through the hole in the trunk, and suddenly found himself in the wide passage, lighted up by many hundred lamps, as the witch had described.

He opened the first door. Bravo! There sat the dog with eyes as large as tea-cups, staring at him as though in utter amazement.

"There's a good creature!" quoth the soldier, as he spread the witch's apron on the floor, and lifted the dog upon it. He then filled his pockets with the copper coins in the chest, shut the lid, put the dog back into his place, and passed on into the second apartment.

Huzza! There sat the dog with eyes as large as mill-wheels.

"You had really better not stare at me so," remarked the soldier; "it will make your eyes weak!" and herewith he set the dog down on the witch's apron. But when, on raising the lid of the chest, he beheld the vast quantity of silver money it contained, he threw all his pence away in disgust, and hastened to fill his pockets and his knapsack with the pure silver. And he passed on into the third chamber. Now, indeed, that was terrifying! The dog in this chamber actually had a pair of eyes each as large as the Round Tower, and they kept rolling round and round in his head like wheels.

"Good evening!" said the soldier, and he lifted his cap respectfully, for such a monster of a dog as this he had never in his life before seen or heard of. He stood still for a minute or two, looking at him, then thinking, "the sooner it's done the better!" He took hold of the immense creature, removed him from the chest to the floor, and raised the lid of the chest. Oh, what a sight of gold was there! enough

173

*...they kept rolling round and round in his head
like wheels*

to buy not only all Copenhagen, but all the cakes and sugar-plums, all the tin soldiers, whips and rocking-horses in the world! Yes, he must be satisfied now. Hastily the soldier threw out all the silver money he had stuffed into his pockets and knapsack, and took gold instead; not only his pockets and knapsack, but his soldier's cap and boots he crammed full of gold, bright gold! heavy gold! he could hardly walk for the weight he carried. He lifted the dog on the chest again, banged the door of the room behind him, and called out through the tree:

"Hello, you old witch! pull me up again!"

"Have you got the tinder-box?" asked the witch.

"Upon my honour, I'd quite forgotten it!" shouted the soldier, and back he went to fetch it. The witch then drew him up through the tree, and now he again stood in the high road, his pockets, boots, knapsack, and cap, stuffed with gold pieces.

"Just tell me now, what are you going to do with the tinder-box?" inquired the soldier.

"That's no concern of yours," returned the witch. "You've got your money; give me my tinder-box this instant!"

"Well, take your choice," said the soldier. "Either tell me at once what you want with the tinder-box, or I draw my sword, and cut off your head."

"I won't tell you!" screamed the witch.

So the soldier drew his sword and cut off her head. There she lay; but he did not waste time in looking at what he had done; he made haste to knot all his money securely in the witch's blue apron, made a bundle of it, and slung it across his back, put the tinder-box into his pocket, and went straight to the nearest town.

It was a large, handsome town; a city, in fact. He walked into the first hotel in the place, called for the best rooms, and ordered the choicest and most expensive dishes for his supper, for he was now a rich man, with plenty of gold to spend.

The servant who cleaned the boots could not help thinking they were disgracefully shabby and worn to belong to such a grand gentleman; however, next day he provided himself with new boots and very gay clothes besides. Our soldier was now a great man, and the people of the hotel were called in to give him information about all the places of amusement in the city, and about their King, and the beautiful Princess, his daughter.

"I should rather like to see her!" observed the soldier; "just tell me when I can?"

"No one can see her at all," was the reply; "she dwells in a great copper palace, with ever so many walls and towers round it. No one but the King may go and visit her there, because it has been foretold that she will marry a common soldier, and our King would not like that at all."

"Shouldn't I like to see her though, just for once!" thought the soldier, but it was of no use for him to wish it.

And now he lived such a merry life! went continually to the theatre, drove out in the Royal Gardens, and gave so much money in alms to the poor—to all, in fact, who asked him. And this was well done in him; to be sure, he knew by past experience how miserable it was not to have a shilling in one's pocket. He was always gaily dressed, and had such a crowd of friends, who, one and all, declared he was a most capital fellow, a real gentleman; and that pleased our soldier uncommonly. But, as he was now giving and spending every day, and never received anything in return, his money began to fail him, and at last he had only twopence left, and was forced to remove from the splendid apartments where he had lodged hitherto, and take refuge in a little bit of an attic-chamber, where he had to brush his boots and darn his clothes himself, and where none of his friends ever came to see him, because there were so many stairs to go up, it was quite fatiguing.

It was a very dark evening, and he could not afford to buy himself so much as a rushlight; however, he remembered, all at once, that there were a few matches lying in the tinder-box that the old witch had bade him fetch out of the hollow tree. So he brought out this tinder-box and began to strike a light; but no sooner had he rubbed the flint-stone and made the sparks fly out than the door burst suddenly open, and the dog with eyes as large as tea-cups, and which he had seen in the cavern beneath the tree, stood before him and said, "What commands has my master for his slave?"

"Upon my honour, this is a pretty joke!" cried the soldier; "a fine sort of tinder-box this is, if it will really provide me with whatever I want. Fetch me some money this instant!" said he to the dog; whereupon the creature vanished, and lo! in half a minute he was back again, holding in his mouth a large bag full of pence.

So now the soldier understood the rare virtue of this charming tinder-box. If he struck the flint only once, the dog that sat on the chest full of copper came to him; if he struck it twice, the dog that watched over the silver answered his summons; and if he struck it three times, he was forthwith attended by the monstrous guardian of the golden treasure.

The soldier could now remove back to his princely apartments, he bought himself an entirely new suit of clothes, and all his friends remembered him again, and loved him as much as ever. But one evening the thought occurred to him, "How truly ridiculous it is that no one should be allowed to see this Princess! They all say she is so very beautiful; what a shame it is that she should be shut up in that great copper palace with the towers guarding it round! And I do so want to see her—where's my tinder-box, by-the-bye?" He struck the flint, and lo! before him stood the dog with eyes as large as tea-cups.

"It is rather late, I must own," began the soldier; "but I do want to see the Princess so much, only for one minute, you know!"

And the dog was out of the door, and, before the soldier had time to think of what he should say or do, he was back again with the Princess sitting asleep on his back. A real Princess was this! so beautiful, so enchantingly beautiful! the soldier could not help himself, he knelt down and kissed her hand.

The dog ran back to the palace with the Princess that very minute; however, next morning while she was at breakfast with the King and Queen, the Princess said that she had had such a strange dream during the past night. She had dreamt that she was riding on a dog, an enormously large dog, and that a soldier had knelt down to her, and kissed her hand.

"A pretty sort of a dream, indeed!" exclaimed the Queen.

And she insisted that one of the old ladies of the court should watch by the Princess's bedside on the following night, in case she should again be disturbed by dreams.

The soldier longed so exceedingly to see the fair Princess of the copper palace again; accordingly, next evening, the dog was summoned to fetch her. So he did, and ran as fast as be could; however, not so fast but that the ancient dame watching at the Princess's couch found time to put on a pair of waterproof boots before running after them. She saw the dog vanish in a large house; then, thinking to herself, "Now I know what to do," she took out a piece of chalk and made a great white cross on the door. She then went home and betook herself to rest, and the Princess was home almost as soon. But on his way the dog chanced to observe the white cross on the door of the hotel where the soldier lived; so he immediately took another piece of chalk and set crosses on every door throughout the town. And this was wisely done on his part.

Early in the morning came out the King, the Queen, the old Court dame, and all the officers of the royal household, every one of them curious to see where the Princess had been.

"Here it is!" exclaimed the King, as soon as he saw the first street-door with a cross chalked on it.

"My dear, where are your eyes?—this is the house," cried the Queen, seeing the second door bear a cross.

"No, this is it surely—why, here's a cross too!" cried all of them together, on discovering that there were crosses on all the doors. It was evident that their search would be in vain, and they were obliged to give it up.

But the Queen was an exceedingly wise and prudent woman; she was good for something besides sitting in a state carriage, and looking very grand and condescending. She now took her gold scissors, cut a large piece of silk stuff into strips and sewed these strips together, to make a pretty, neat little bag. This bag she filled with the finest, whitest flour, and with her own hands tied it to the Princess's waist, and when this was done, again took up her golden scissors and cut a little hole in the bag, just large enough to let the flour drop out gradually all the time the Princess was moving.

That evening the dog came again, took the Princess on his back, and ran away with her to the soldier. Oh, how the soldier loved her, and how he wished he were a prince, that he might have this beautiful Princess for his wife!

The dog never perceived how the flour went drip, drip, dripping, all the way from the palace to the soldier's room, and from the soldier's room back to the palace. So next morning the King and Queen could easily discover where their daughter had been carried, and they took the soldier and cast him into prison.

And now he sat in the prison. Oh! how dark it was, and how wearisome! and the turnkey kept coming in to remind him that tomorrow he was to be hanged. This piece of news was by no means agreeable; and the tinder-box had been left in his lodgings at the hotel.

When morning came, he could, through his narrow iron grating, watch the people all hurrying out of the town to see him hanged; he could hear the drums beating, and presently, too, he saw the soldiers marching to the place of execution. What a crowd there was rushing by! among the rest was a shoemaker's apprentice in his leathern apron and slippers; he bustled on with such speed that one of his slippers flew off and bounded against the iron staves of the soldier's prison window.

"Stop, stop, little 'prentice!" cried the soldier; "it's of no use for you to be in such a hurry, for none of the fun will begin till I come, but if you'll oblige me by running to my lodgings and fetching me my tinder-box, I'll give you twopence. But you must run for your life!" The shoemaker's boy liked the idea of earning twopence, so away he raced after the tinder-box, returned, and gave it to the soldier, and then—ah, yes, now we shall hear what happened then.

Outside the city a gibbet had been erected; round it were marshalled the soldiers with many hundred thousand people, men, women, and children; the King and Queen were seated on magnificent thrones, exactly opposite the judges and the whole assembled council.

Already had the soldier mounted the topmost step of the ladder; already was the executioner on the point of fitting the rope round his neck, when, turning to their Majesties, he began to entreat most earnestly that they would suffer a poor criminal's innocent fancy to be gratified before he underwent his punishment. He wished so much, he said, to smoke a pipe of tobacco, and as it was the last pleasure he could enjoy in this world, he hoped it would not be denied him.

The King could not refuse this harmless request, accordingly the soldier took out his tinder-box and struck the flint—once he struck it, twice he struck it, three times he struck it!—and lo! all the three wizard dogs stood before him, the dog with eyes as large as tea-cups, the dog with eyes as large as mill-wheels, and the dog with eyes each as large as the Round Tower!

"Now, help me, don't let me be hanged!" cried the soldier. And forthwith the three terrible dogs fell upon the judges and councillors, tossing them high into the air, so high that on falling down to the ground again they were broken in pieces.

"We will not——" began the king, but the monster dog with eyes as large as the Round Tower did not wait to hear what his Majesty would not; he seized both him and the Queen, and flung them up into the air after the councillors. And the soldiers were all desperately frightened, and the people shouted out with one voice, "Good soldier, you shall be our King, and the beautiful Princess shall be your wife, and our Queen!"

So the soldier was conducted into the royal carriage, and all the three dogs bounded to and fro in front, little boys whistled upon their fingers, and the guards presented arms. The Princess was forthwith sent for and made Queen, which she liked much better than living a prisoner in the copper palace. The bridal festivities lasted for eight whole days, and the three wizard dogs sat at the banquet-table, staring about them with their great eyes.

THE RED SHOES

THERE was once a little girl, very pretty and delicate, but so poor that in summer time she always went barefoot, and in winter wore large wooden shoes, so that her little ankles grew quite red and sore.

In the village dwelt the shoemaker's mother. She sat down one day and made out of some old pieces of red cloth a pair of little shoes; they were clumsy enough, certainly, but they fitted the little girl tolerably well, and she gave them to her. The little girl's name was Karen.

It was the day of her mother's funeral when the red shoes were given to Karen; they were not at all suitable for mourning, but she had no others, and in them she walked with bare legs behind the miserable straw bier.

Just then a large old carriage rolled by; in it sat a large old lady; she looked at the little girl and pitied her, and she said to the priest, "Give me the little girl and I will take care of her."

And Karen thought it was all for the sake of the red shoes that the old lady had taken this fancy to her, but the old lady said they were frightful, and they were burnt. And Karen was dressed very neatly; she was taught to read and to work; and people told her she was pretty—but the mirror said, "Thou art more than pretty, thou art beautiful!"

It happened one day that the Queen travelled through that part of the country with her little daughter, the Princess; and all the people, Karen amongst them, crowded in front of the palace, whilst the little Princess stood, dressed in white, at a window, for every one to see her. She wore neither train nor gold crown; but on her feet were pretty red morocco shoes, much prettier ones indeed than those the shoemaker's mother had made for little Karen. Nothing in the world could be compared to these red shoes.

Karen was now old enough to be confirmed, she was to have both new frock and new shoes. The rich shoemaker in the town took the measure of her little foot. Large glass cases full of neat shoes and shining boots were fixed round the room; however, the old lady's sight was not very good, and, naturally enough, she had not so much pleasure in looking at them as Karen had. Amongst the shoes was a pair of red ones, just like those worn by the Princess. How gay they were! and the shoemaker said they had been made for a count's daughter, but had not quite fitted her.

"They are of polished leather," said the old lady, "see how they shine!"

"Yes, they shine beautifully!" exclaimed Karen. And as the shoes fitted her, they were bought; but the old lady did not know that they were red, for she would never have suffered Karen to go to confirmation in red shoes. But Karen did so. Everybody looked at her feet, and as she walked up the nave to the chancel, it seemed to her that even the antique sculptured figures on the monuments, with their stiff ruffs and long black robes, fixed their eyes on her red shoes. Of them only she thought when the Bishop laid his hand on her head, when he spoke of Holy Baptism, of her covenant with God, and how she must now be a full-grown Christian. The organ sent forth its deep, solemn tones, the children's sweet voices mingled with those of the choristers, but Karen still thought only of her red shoes.

That afternoon, when the old lady was told that Karen had worn red shoes at her confirmation, she was much vexed, and told Karen that they were quite unsuitable, and that, hence-forward, whenever she went to church, she must wear black shoes, were they ever so old.

Next Sunday was the communion day. Karen looked first at the red shoes, then at the black ones, then at the red again, and—put them on.

It was beautiful sunshiny weather; Karen and the old lady walked to church through the corn-fields; the path was very dusty.

At the church door stood an old soldier; he was leaning on crutches, and had a marvellously long beard, not white, but reddish-hued, and he bowed almost to the earth, and asked the old lady if he might wipe the dust off her shoes. And Karen put out her little foot also. "Oh, what pretty dancing-shoes!" quoth the old soldier; "take care, and mind you do not let them slip off when you dance;" and he passed his hands over them.

The old lady gave the soldier a halfpenny, and then went with Karen into church.

And every one looked at Karen's red shoes; and all the carved figures, too, bent their gaze upon them; and when Karen knelt before the altar, the red shoes still floated before her eyes, she thought of them and of them only, and she forgot to join in the hymn of praise— she forgot to repeat "Our Father".

At last all the people came out of church, and the old lady got into her carriage. Karen was just lifting her foot to follow her, when the old soldier standing in the porch exclaimed. "Only look, what pretty dancing-shoes!" And Karen could not help it, she felt she must make a few of her dancing steps; and after she had once begun, her feet continued to move, just as though the shoes had received power over them; she danced round the churchyard, she could not stop. The coachman was obliged to run after her; he took hold of her and lifted her into the carriage, but the feet still continued to dance, so as to kick the good old lady most cruelly. At last the shoes were taken off, and the feet had the rest which they needed.

And now the shoes were put away in a press, but Karen could not help going to look at them every now and then.

The old lady lay ill in bed; the doctor said she could not live much longer. She certainly needed careful nursing, and who should be her nurse and constant attendant but Karen? But there was to be a grand ball in the town, Karen was invited; she looked at the old lady, who was almost dying—she looked at the red shoes—she put them on, there could be no harm in doing that, at least; she went to the ball, and began to dance. But when she wanted to move to the right, the shoes bore her to the left; and when she would dance up the room, the shoes danced down the room, danced down the stairs, through the streets, and through the gates of the town. Dance she did, and dance she must, straight out into the dark wood.

Something all at once shone through the trees. She thought at first it must be the moon's bright face, shining blood-red through the night mists; but no, it was the old soldier with the red beard—he sat there, nodding at her, and repeating, "Only look, what pretty dancing-shoes!"

She was very much frightened, and tried to throw off her red shoes, but could not unclasp them. She hastily tore off her stockings, but the shoes she could not get rid of—they had, it seemed, grown on to her feet. Dance she did, and dance she must, over field and meadow, in rain and in sunshine, by night and by day—by night! that was most horrible! She danced into the lonely churchyard, but the dead there danced not, they were at rest. She would fain have sat down on the poor man's grave, where the bitter tansy grew, but for her there was neither rest nor respite. She danced past the open church door; there she saw an angel, clad in long white robes, and with wings that reached from his shoulders to the earth; his countenance was grave and stern, and in his hand he held a broad glittering sword.

"Dance thou shalt," said he; "dance on, in thy red shoes, till thou

184

She tried to throw off her red shoes

art pale and cold, and thy skin shrinks and crumples up like a skeleton's! Dance thou shalt still, from door to door, and wherever proud, vain children live thou shalt knock, so that they may hear thee and fear! Dance shalt thou, dance on——"

"Mercy!" cried Karen; but she heard not the angel's answer, for the shoes carried her through the gate, into the fields, along highways and byways, and still she must dance.

One morning she danced past a door she knew well; she heard psalm-singing from within, and presently a coffin, strewn with flowers, was borne out. Then Karen knew that the good old lady was dead, and she felt herself a thing forsaken by all mankind, and accursed by the Angel of God.

Dance she did, and dance she must, even through the dark night; the shoes bore her continually over thorns and briers, till her limbs were torn and bleeding. Away she danced over the heath to a little solitary house; she knew that the headsman dwelt there, and she tapped with her fingers against the panes, crying—

"Come out! come out!—I cannot come in to you, I am dancing."

And the headsman replied, "Surely thou knowest not who I am. I cut off the heads of wicked men, and my axe is very sharp and keen."

"Cut not off my head!" said Karen! "for then I could not live to repent of my sin; but cut off my feet with the red shoes."

And then she confessed to him all her sin, and the headsman cut off her feet with the red shoes on them; but even after this the shoes still danced away with those little feet over the fields, and into the deep forests.

And the headsman made her a pair of wooden feet, and hewed down some boughs to serve her as crutches, and he taught her the psalm which is always repeated by criminals, and she kissed the hand that had guided the axe, and went her way over the heath. "Now I have certainly suffered quite enough through the red shoes," thought Karen, "I will go to church and let people see me once more!" and she went as fast as she could to the church porch, but as she approached it, the red shoes danced before her, and she was frightened and turned her back.

All that week through she endured the keenest anguish and shed many bitter tears; however, when Sunday came, she said to herself, "Well, I must have suffered and striven enough by this time, I dare say I am quite as good as many of those who are holding their heads so high in church." So she took courage and went there, but she had not passed the churchyard gate before she saw the red shoes again dancing before her, and in great terror she again turned back, and more deeply than ever bewailed her sin.

She then went to the pastor's house, and begged that some employment might be given her, promising to work diligently and do all she could; she did not wish for any wages, she said, she only wanted a roof to shelter her, and to dwell with good people. And the pastor's wife had pity on her, and took her into her service. And Karen was grateful and industrious.

Every evening she sat silently listening to the pastor, while he read the Holy Scriptures aloud. All the children loved her, but when she heard them talk about dress and finery, and about being as beautiful as a queen, she would sorrowfully shake her head.

Again Sunday came, all the pastor's household went to church, and they asked her if she would not go too, but she sighed and looked with tears in her eyes upon her crutches.

When they were all gone, she went into her own little, lowly chamber—it was but just large enough to contain a bed and chair—and there she sat down with her psalm-book in her hand, and whilst she was meekly and devoutly reading in it, the wind wafted the tones of the organ from the church into her room, and she lifted up her face to heaven and prayed, with tears, "O God, help me!"

Then the sun shone brightly, so brightly!—and behold! close before her stood the white-robed Angel of God, the same whom she had seen on that night of horror at the church porch, but his hand wielded not now, as then, a sharp, threatening sword—he held a lovely green bough, full of roses. With this he touched the ceiling, which immediately rose to a great height, a bright gold star spangling in the spot where the Angel's green bough had touched it. And he touched the walls, whereupon the room widened, and Karen saw the organ, the old monuments, and the congregation all sitting in their richly-carved seats and singing from their psalm-books.

For the church had come home to the poor girl in her narrow chamber, or rather the chamber had grown, as it were, into the church; she sat with the rest of the pastor's household, and, when the psalm was ended, they looked up and nodded to her, saying, "Thou didst well to come, Karen!"

"This is mercy!" said she.

And the organ played again, and the children's voices in the choir mingled so sweetly and plaintively with it! The bright sunbeams streamed warmly through the windows upon Karen's seat; her heart was so full of sunshine, of peace and gladness, that it broke; her soul flew upon a sunbeam to her Father in heaven, where not a look of reproach awaited her, not a word was breathed of the red shoes.